Cold metal touch

"There is nothing I would like more than to kill you, but Carlos wants you for himself."

The elevator car climbed slowly. Bolan stood with his arms outstretched, his palms against the doors. He could see the control panel near his left hand and the red button that meant the difference between his life and death. When Scarface glanced up at the floor-indicator arrow, the Executioner made his move.

The Brazilian tried to get off a shot, but the jolt of the car lurching to a halt threw him against the rear wall. Bolan turned and pistoned his knee into his enemy's chest, dazing him. He followed up with a chop to the wrist, forcing the man to drop his weapon.

Scarface was tough. He absorbed the punch without flinching, shifted and suddenly had a 9 mm automatic in his hand. His scar flushed red with anger, he lunged, pressed the muzzle of the gun to the warrior's chest and squeezed the trigger.

MACK BOLAN®

The Executioner

DON PENDLETON'S
THE EXECUTIONER®
FEATURING MACK BOLAN®

EXTREME FORCE

A GOLD EAGLE BOOK FROM
WORLDWIDE®

TORONTO • NEW YORK • LONDON
AMSTERDAM • PARIS • SYDNEY • HAMBURG
STOCKHOLM • ATHENS • TOKYO • MILAN
MADRID • WARSAW • BUDAPEST • AUCKLAND

First edition November 1994

ISBN 0-373-61191-9

Special thanks and acknowledgment to
David Robbins for his contribution to this work.

EXTREME FORCE

Tyranny, like hell, is not easily conquered.
—Thomas Paine

This world is filled with unprincipled power mongers who think they can inflict untold agonies on the innocent with impunity. I've devoted my life to showing them how very wrong they are.
—Mack Bolan

THE
MACK BOLAN®
LEGEND

Nothing less than a war could have fashioned the destiny of the man called Mack Bolan. Bolan earned the Executioner title in the jungle hell of Vietnam.

But this soldier also wore another name—Sergeant Mercy. He was so tagged because of the compassion he showed to wounded comrades-in-arms and Vietnamese civilians.

Mack Bolan's second tour of duty ended prematurely when he was given emergency leave to return home and bury his family, victims of the Mob. Then he declared a one-man war against the Mafia.

He confronted the Families head-on from coast to coast, and soon a hope of victory began to appear. But Bolan had broken society's every rule. That same society started gunning for this elusive warrior—to no avail.

So Bolan was offered amnesty to work within the system against terrorism. This time, as an employee of Uncle Sam, Bolan became Colonel John Phoenix. With a command center at Stony Man Farm in Virginia, he and his new allies—Able Team and Phoenix Force—waged relentless war on a new adversary: the KGB.

But when his one true love, April Rose, died at the hands of the Soviet terror machine, Bolan severed all ties with Establishment authority.

Now, after a lengthy lone-wolf struggle and much soul-searching, the Executioner has agreed to enter an "arm's-length" alliance with his government once more, reserving the right to pursue personal missions in his Everlasting War.

PROLOGUE

Death stalked Capitol Hill. It came in the guise of ten men who had vowed to bring the United States of America to its knees, who had pledged their lives to the cause of crippling the Great Satanic Empire. On a cold, blustery day on which the Senate was in earnest debate, they struck.

No one paid any attention as Yusuf Atasi, alias Tony Bianco, went about his menial tasks. But then, no one ever paid any attention to the janitorial staff. They were permitted to make their rounds without interference.

Atasi stopped at a utility closet. Slipping inside, he positioned a small stepladder below an air vent and climbed up. A screwdriver enabled him to pry the vent open. He had to tug to lift the heavy duffel bag that had taken all the ingenuity the Golden Scimitar could muster to smuggle into the building.

Working rapidly, Atasi laid out the contents. When the bag was empty, he consulted his watch. The last tour group of the day was supposed to be at the Grand Staircase-East. Rising, Atasi peeked out. When the hall was clear he closed and locked the door, then hastened off.

Hasham, Adib, Sami and Shukri were tailing the tour group, pretending to be interested in the architecture. The instant they saw Atasi, they veered into the side corridor. No one else even noticed. Without saying a word the terrorist led them back the way he had come.

Atasi unlocked the utility closet, then kept watch while the four men took turns claiming weapons and stuffing spare magazines and grenades into their pockets. "Hurry!" he commanded in Arabic. "Abdul and the others will create the diversion in two minutes."

Entering last, Atasi slung a Heckler & Koch MP-5 over his right arm and an Uzi over his left. Two grenades completed his hardware. He checked his watch again. "Let's go."

Explosions thundered in the distance as Atasi barreled down the plush corridor. There were faint shouts and screams. People began to step out of doorways and to look around in concern. Atasi shoved them out of his way, ignoring their squeals of protest or their oaths. He turned another corner, hurried past the Marble Room and the President's Room, which was vacant, as he had known it would be.

During the three months Atasi had worked at the Capitol, he had learned its layout from top to bottom. He knew which corridors were used the most, and when. He knew where the guards were stationed, knew when they changed shifts. In short, he had learned every detail essential for the success of their operation.

The Senate Chamber came into sight, and Atasi picked up the pace. Seconds later they burst in on the august body to find anxious senators milling about in confusion, and opened fire.

It was a slaughter. Atasi smiled broadly as he poured a withering burst of 9 mm lead into the ranks of the defenseless politicians. Pulling a grenade, he yanked the pin, lobbed the bomb into their midst and flattened behind the last row of seats as the explosion rocked the walls. There were shrieks of torment and wails of agony.

Atasi got up, steadied the Uzi and resumed firing. He saw some senators and aides fleeing out doorways and cursed under his breath.

His group had to work quickly in order to be in and out of the chamber within a minute and a half. As much as Atasi would have liked to wipe out the entire Senate, he had no wish to be a martyr. This wasn't a suicide attack. He wanted to live on to carry on the good fight, to inflict as much damage as he could to the imperialist pigs before they took him out.

The magazine ran dry, and rather than replace it, Atasi promptly switched from the Uzi to the MP-5. As he did, he glanced to his right and saw Sami go down with a bullet between the eyes. Without thinking, he went to place a hand on his friend's shoulder, then recoiled when a slug ripped into the floor inches from his fingers.

Pivoting, Atasi scanned the chamber and spotted a uniform with a badge attached. He tilted the submachine gun and stroked the trigger just as the man prepared to fire. The terrorist grinned when his target flew backward to land in a crumpled heap.

Those senators not wounded or dead had sought cover. Atasi glimpsed a head poking above a seat and snapped off several shots. The head stayed down.

Adib and Shukri raced down the aisle, seeking more victims.

Suddenly a new element was added. Five D.C. cops burst through a far doorway, their service revolvers drawn. They began shooting as soon as they laid eyes on the two men, and Shukri went down.

Atasi, enraged, turned the MP-5 on the newcomers, but they hit the floor before he could achieve target acquisition. He couldn't believe the turn of events. There weren't supposed to be any cops anywhere in the vicinity.

"Time!" Hasham bellowed.

Cursing, Atasi fired a barrage at the police officers to keep them pinned down while Adib retreated up the aisle. A young, reckless cop jumped up, and Atasi cored him through the shoulder—but not before the man nailed Adib squarely between the shoulder blades. Spurting blood, the terrorist collapsed.

Atasi would have rushed to Adib had Hasham not grabbed his arm and hustled him from the chamber. In the hallway pandemonium reigned. People were running every which way. Those who saw the weapons the two terrorists carried cowered against the wall or ducked with their hands over their heads.

Atasi was in a livid funk. He wanted to kill them all, to slay every last American who lived.

"We must hurry if we are to reach the van in time," Hasham said.

The reminder jarred Atasi into realizing he might well share the fate of his slain comrades if he didn't vacate the Capitol, and quickly. He came to an empty room and pulled Hasham in after him. In no time they discarded their hardware.

The gunfire and explosions had sparked a mass exodus. Frightened workers and visitors alike were streaming along the main corridors and out into the bright afternoon sunlight. It was an easy matter for Atasi and Hasham to join the panicked throngs.

Once in the parking lot, the terrorist leader twisted for a look at the Capitol dome. There was a gaping, jagged hole halfway up. Several of the Corinthian columns had been shattered and lay in ruins. Smoke poured from the South Small Rotunda.

The van was idling right where it should be. Atasi let Hasham scurry into the back with the four men waiting there, then he took a seat across from the driver, Abdul. "You did well."

"The LAWs worked as we were promised," Abdul replied. He looked out the window. "Where are the rest?"

Atasi frowned. "They have paid the supreme price. But they will be avenged, my friend." He glared as police cars rushed by with sirens blaring and lights flashing and screeched to a stop at the base of the high steps.

The van pulled from its parking space. Atasi shook a fist at the Statue of Freedom atop the ravaged dome and swore. "We will bring you down," he vowed. "We will destroy this wicked country and all it stands for! Mark my words!"

As more and more cruisers roared into the parking lot, the brown van blended into the flow of traffic and was soon lost in the afternoon haze.

1

Mack Bolan, a.k.a. the Executioner, stood on a windswept knoll a hundred yards from a dark farmhouse, studying the building through the Starlite scope mounted on his M-16. He was dressed for action in a combat blacksuit, its many pockets filled with the weapons of war he might need. Under his left arm was a Beretta 93-R, on his right hip a powerful .44 Desert Eagle.

The farmhouse appeared empty but wasn't, according to the latest intel. Hal Brognola, director of the Justice Department's Sensitive Operations Group, had assured Bolan that those responsible for the attack on the Capitol three days earlier were holed up at this remote spot in rural Virginia.

Bolan hoped that the big Fed was right. He wanted to bring down the butchers who called themselves Golden Scimitar, to see them pay for the atrocities they had committed in the name of Islamic fundamentalism.

The attack on the U.S. Senate was but the latest in a long string of bloodbaths. Nine senators had died, twelve had been wounded. Fourteen aides and clerks had perished, and twice as many would be in the hospital for weeks, if not months. The damage to the Capitol itself ran into the millions.

Few terrorist onslaughts had so jolted America as this one. It was worse than the World Trade Center bombing, worse than any overseas incident, simply because Golden Scimitar had struck at the very heart of all that America stood for and all that stood for America.

To a man like Mack Bolan, who fought the viperous scourge of terrorism wherever it reared its vicious head, the shocking news had been like a physical blow to the gut. He'd contacted Brognola, asking for any additional information the big Fed could come up with.

Brognola had been all too happy to comply, and the warrior had found himself in an unmarked helicopter speeding south within the hour.

There was, however, one hitch. Based on the weapons used by the dead terrorists and whispers in the intelligence community, the Feds had reason to believe that Golden Scimitar had ties to an illicit arms dealer that Brognola had been trying to put out of operation for some time. So now the Justice man wanted at least one of the fanatics taken alive.

Hefting the M-16, Bolan crouched and padded down the knoll into a wooded tract. It had rained earlier and the grass was slick. He had to be careful not to slip.

A log offered a convenient spot to again train the Starlite scope on the house. Built more than a hundred years earlier, it was three stories high and surrounded by overgrown lilac bushes and shrubbery. The third-story windows gave the terrorists a clear field of fire, and the dense shrubbery offered plenty of places for a lookout to hide.

Bolan didn't like the setup, but he had no choice. There would never be a better time to go in. Low clouds and lingering wisps of fog worked in his favor.

Staying bent at the waist, the warrior glided around the log and went from tree to tree, his ears straining to catch the faintest sounds. There were crickets galore, and off in the trees an owl hooted. All seemed peaceful. Perhaps too peaceful.

Twenty yards from the house the warrior crouched behind a maple tree. He detected a faint pale glow along the edges of a window on the second floor, proving there was definitely someone in there. The terrorists, he guessed, had the windows covered so no one could see in.

Bolan was about to sprint to a nearby bush when he noticed a tiny red dot on his chest. His reaction was to hurl himself to the right and flatten. He did so with not a moment to spare, as a gunner in the shrubbery cut loose with a burst of autofire.

The warrior rolled to the left until he came up against another tree. Pushing up onto one knee, he surveyed the foliage. A laser sight was more than he had bargained on. The opposition, apparently, had more sophisticated arms than he had been led to believe.

Abruptly a pencil-thin crimson beam stabbed the night off to the right. The terrorist had made a grave mistake, because Bolan had only to trace the beam back to its source to pinpoint where the gunner was hiding. That was the one drawback to laser sights and why Bolan hardly ever used them; they increased accuracy at the expense of concealment.

The warrior fixed the Starlite scope on a shrub and found his man squatting at its base. His first impulse was to go for a head shot, then he remembered that Brognola needed a few of the terrorists alive. Reluctantly he lowered the cross hairs and put a single round through the terrorist's shoulder.

Someone shouted in Arabic. "Over here! Over here!" Footsteps pounded in the night.

Bolan spied vague figures angling toward him and hugged the dank earth. Muzzle-flashes winked in the darkness, then heavy-caliber rounds ate into the trunk, chipping off bark.

Scrambling to one side, the Executioner crawled behind a bush. He unclipped a stun grenade and focused on two shadows converging from the northeast. When they were close enough, he threw the lethal egg. The concussion knocked them both down, but Bolan had no way of knowing if they were out.

He darted to the right, knowing he was outnumbered and on unfamiliar ground. In order to keep the hardmen on the defensive he had to keep on the move.

Bolan also needed to disable their getaway vehicle. He hadn't seen one so far, but there was a shed large enough to harbor a car or truck at one corner of the house. That became his next priority, and he was within a few yards of his goal when all hell broke loose.

A commotion erupted inside, muted voices and a loud thud, as if a car door were closing. An engine roared to life, shaking the shed on its foundation. Tires squealed, and without warning the door buckled outward with a tremendous crash as an old four-door sedan smashed through.

With inches to spare Bolan leaped aside. Spinning, he aimed at the shadowy outline of the driver and squeezed off a short burst. The car's window dissolved in a spray of glass, and a strident blare sounded as the driver slumped over the steering wheel. Out of control, the sedan plowed into a pine tree.

One other terrorist jumped from the passenger-side door and made for the woods, firing on the run.

So much for taking Golden Scimitar alive, Bolan reflected grimly as he ducked behind the shed. One was already dead and three were wounded. The rest would be fanning out to catch him in a pincer movement. These men were professionals and wouldn't miss a trick.

The warrior raced to the trees. A low branch gave him an idea and he leaped as he went under, grabbing hold so he could pull himself up and straddle the branch.

Any good hunter knew that deer and other game rarely bothered to raise their eyes above ground level, which explained why many a sportsman liked to pick off his quarry from a roost high in a tree. The same trait applied to human prey, and Bolan counted on that fact to further reduce the odds.

Balancing on his stomach, the Executioner went as rigid as the branch. No sooner had he done so than crackling arose in a thicket to his right. Shortly a stocky shape emerged.

Bolan knew better than to rivet his eyes on the killer; sometimes that alone was enough to forewarn anyone with combat-heightened senses. Instead, he watched the man approach out of the corner of his eye.

The terrorist would take a few steps, then stop and nervously look around. It was as if his intuition was warning him that something was wrong.

Tensing, the warrior held his breath as the man walked directly underneath him. All Bolan had to do was slide off the branch and ram the stock of the M-16 into the terrorist's skull. But just as he let go, the man looked up, then started to leap aside. The stock only clipped him, sending him sprawling, dazed but not unconscious.

Swinging the M-16 had thrown Bolan slightly off balance, enough for his right ankle to buckle as he came down. He was at arm's length from the terrorist as the man brought an Enfield assault rifle to bear. Taking him alive would be impossible. It was either kill or be killed.

At point-blank range the M-16 chattered, the slugs stitching an uneven path from the man's navel to his neck. The impact flung him to the grass where he convulsed briefly and was still.

Bolan was on the move before his finger eased up on the trigger. He plunged into the vegetation to crouch and listen intently. Satisfied it was safe, he headed northward, toward the spot where he had downed the pair of gunners with a stun grenade. If they were still out, he could bind them and drag them off into the brush until he finished with the others. That way Brognola would get at least two live ones.

The warrior had gone less than thirty feet when his attention was arrested by movement near the house. Freezing, he distinguished the profile of a man shuffling slowly toward a door. The figure had a hand pressed to one shoulder and appeared to be unarmed.

Bolan angled to intercept him. Here was a chance to bag number three and glean a little helpful intel at the same time. The warrior touched the muzzle of the M-16 to the wounded terrorist's back as the man's hand closed on the doorknob. "Don't twitch a muscle," Bolan whispered.

The terrorist stiffened.

"Inside, quick. And keep those hands where I can see them." Bolan kept the muzzle pressed against the man's flesh. Within was a small empty room. Another door, partially open, led into a murky narrow hall. Bolan gave the terrorist a light push into a corner, then stepped back against the opposite wall so he could cover the man and both doors at the same time. "Name?" he snapped quietly.

"Hasham Shishakly."

"If you tell me the truth, you live. If you don't, you die. It's as simple as that."

"I have decided I do not want to die as much as I believed I did."

"How many of you are there?"

"Eight, counting Jabal."

"Who?"

"Our contact on the freighter that is to take us to South America. He is not here at present."

The warrior did some fast calculating. "I told you what would happen if you lied," he said, elevating the M-16.

"But I didn't!"

Bolan hesitated. There was an outside chance the terrorist was telling the truth. Which meant there were three hardmen still out there somewhere.

Suddenly the night was shattered by automatic fire. Rounds ripped through the frame walls and the door, pouring from several directions at once, peppering the room. Bolan went prone at the first shot.

The terrorist's reflexes weren't as razor sharp. He cried out as slugs dug into him, catapulting him into the hallway.

A shadow flitted across the outer doorway, and Bolan saw a dark, spherical object land on the floor. He was up in a twinkling, heedless of the blistering fusillade, and racing for the hall. His left elbow was nicked; something plucked at his pants.

A leap carried Bolan over the twitching body. He reached the next room and cut to the right in a running dive, putting the wall between himself and the hall at the same instant the grenade detonated. A gust of air buffeted him as debris spewed into the room.

His ears ringing, the warrior shoved himself erect. There was another hall straight ahead, stairs to his right. He went for the high ground, taking the stairs three at a stride. In the gloom it was hard to see. He stopped shy of the landing, bothered by a thought. There was a chance the terrorists had seen fit to booby-trap the house. He had to be careful, or he could wind up stumbling over a trip wire.

Bolan advanced cautiously. On the landing he paused to examine a window over which newspaper had been taped. He pried at a bottom corner until he loosened the masking tape, then peeked out.

The yard below was deceptively serene. Not so much as a leaf moved.

Sometimes winning a firefight had as much to do with psychology as it did with firepower. Bolan tried to think as the terrorists would think. What would they do next? It was unlikely they would flee, not when they now knew they were up against one man and they had him cornered. It was also unlikely they would try to burn him out, since a fire that size was bound to be spotted by neighboring farmers who would notify the police.

No, if Bolan was in their shoes, he'd do one of two things, either wait for the cornered party to make a break, or send someone into the house after him.

A creak downstairs told the warrior which choice the terrorists had made.

Bolan edged into inky shadows that bordered the landing. He lightly touched his finger to the trigger and waited. Anyone foolhardy enough to come up those steps was going to lose his head. Guaranteed.

Evidently the terrorists were smarter than Bolan had thought. Whoever was on the first floor stayed on the first floor. The warrior could hear someone moving about, and once he heard whispering. Then, for the longest while, all was still.

A check of his watch showed Bolan that it was close to 4:00 a.m. Brognola wouldn't send in a backup team for another two hours. That was about how long it would take for the big Fed to decide that the Executioner was in trouble.

Tired of the stalemate, Bolan went from room to room. In one he found three mats on the floor, in another four more, which tallied with the total number of terrorists according to Shishakly. There were also dozens of empty tin cans and milk cartons scattered about. In a third the warrior discovered piled foodstuffs, enough to last seven men a month or better.

He returned to the window and checked for activity below. There was none, which proved nothing. The terrorists certainly hadn't gone anywhere.

Bolan found it impossible to wait around for the enemy to bring the fight to him. He preferred to be on the offensive. The M-16 at the ready, he took the stairs to the third floor to see what he could find. The ceiling was lower, the rooms clearly meant for small kids. He had to duck low as he went from one to the other. All were empty, all musty with dust.

As the Executioner vacated the last room he heard muted voices. Glancing around, he spotted the source, a vent at floor level. On hands and knees he listened. The conversation was in Arabic, a language he had a passing familiarity with, but he was unable to distinguish enough words to get the gist of what the terrorists were saying.

Standing, Bolan wiped his hands on his blacksuit and turned to go. His eyes happened to drift to the ceiling, to a corner in which a short cord dangled from a hole in a trapdoor. Curious, he walked over, gave the cord a sharp tug and caught the door as it swung open.

There was an attic up above. Bolan jumped, caught the edge with both hands and pulled himself up. A breeze fanned his cheeks. He saw a small window to his right, the glass long since broken out. Going over, he leaned on the jamb.

Very little of the yard and surrounding woods could be seen because the roof blocked his view. He squeezed his shoulders through the opening but still couldn't see. Venturing all the way out, he slid down a short incline to a flat, wide section. Then, easing onto his belly, the big man inched to the very edge.

From this vantage point Bolan could survey the grounds to the south of the house and the woods on either side. The first sight he saw sent a tingle rippling down his spine.

Three figures were sprinting southward. One looked back as they rounded a tree, his teeth flashing white.

The short hairs on Bolan's nape prickled. His combat savvy and his gut instincts told him to get out of there and to get out quickly. He looked over the edge and spied a rainspout to his left. The warrior reached down and gave the spout a tug, testing whether it would hold his weight. The rusty spout creaked, but the supports seemed sturdy enough.

Swiftly Bolan slung the M-16 over his left shoulder, dangled his legs over the rim and proceeded to lower himself. His knees clamped on the spout, and once his hands had a firm purchase he descended.

The night wind brought faint laughter to his ears.

Bolan hurried as best he could. The spout shook with every movement he made, and if he leaned back too far it would sway ominously. He reached the second story and started past a window bordered by black shutters.

Without warning, a squeaking bundle of fur and wings flapped out from behind the shutter, straight at Bolan's face. In sheer reflex he jerked backward and the bat missed him. But in so doing, he put too much pressure on the supports. There was a horrendous metallic grinding noise, and the spout abruptly snapped loose from the wall and tilted outward.

Bolan felt a rush of air as he swooped toward the ground. He retained his grip but his legs slipped off and for a few wild seconds he dangled precariously. The spout unexpectedly bent two-thirds of the way down, then snapped in two. Bolan plummeted.

The warrior concentrated on keeping his legs under him to absorb the brunt of the fall. He looked down, realized that he wasn't going to land on the grass and braced himself just as he crashed into a lilac bush. Branches tore at his clothes, leaves brushed his face and a jarring blow to the ribs made him wince. Then he was tumbling clear of the lilacs and rolling across the overgrown lawn.

Coming to rest against a shrub, Bolan stood and ran. There was no time to take stock, no time for anything except putting as much distance as possible between the house and himself. He raced southward, weaving among trees, vaulting logs, wondering how soon it would be.

The answer came not ten seconds later. As the warrior crossed a clearing, a nova flared to his rear and a massive explosion ripped the farmhouse apart. So great was the blast that the earth shook under Bolan's feet. A wall of hot air slammed into his back, lifting him and throwing him. He landed with such force that the breath whooshed from his lungs. Stunned, he lifted his head and saw a huge cloud of dust and debris. Knowing what would happen next, he scrambled under a pine tree and protectively covered his head with his arms.

Then the deluge commenced. Wood, metal and myriad unrecognizable objects rained from the sky. Some pieces were small, others big enough to crush a person flat. The din was horrendous.

Abruptly all was calm. Bolan lifted his head to find the lawn littered with rubble. A lilac tree not far off had been flattened by part of a wall. A mangled old stove lay upended nearby.

The warrior stood and checked to be sure he hadn't lost the Beretta or the Desert Eagle. Unslinging the M-16, he jogged in pursuit of the surviving members of Golden Scimitar. His legs were unsteady for a few strides before settling down to a smooth rhythm.

The question uppermost on the warrior's mind was, where were the terrorists going? They were out in the middle of nowhere, as it were. The nearest town lay thirty miles to the east. The closest city was twice that distance to the north. So why were they heading south?

Bolan had gone over a mile when he emerged from the woodland to find a recently tilled field and the answer to his question. A quarter of a mile farther stood another farmhouse, a barn and a silo. As he paused momentarily, the night was shattered by automatic gunfire capped by a piercing scream.

Someone was in trouble.

2

Mack Bolan gazed down at the bullet-riddled bodies of an elderly farmer and his gray-haired wife. The pair wore nightshirts, indicating they had been in bed when the terrorists pounded on their door. The man had been gunned down right there in the doorway, his wife apparently when she came to his aid.

Turning, Bolan watched a pair of taillights recede in the darkness. He no longer much cared whether any of Golden Scimitar stayed healthy or not. If they threw down their weapons and fell to their knees when he caught up with them, fine. If not, Hal Brognola would have to track down the illicit arms dealer some other way.

His mouth a somber slash, Bolan ran to the garage flanking the house. One door hung wide, revealing an empty space where the stolen vehicle had sat. He shoved on the second door and discovered an old pickup in tiptop condition. A fresh coat of wax and new tires told of the care the old farmer had given it.

Unfortunately there was no key in the ignition. The Executioner would have to hot-wire the engine to get it started. He'd noticed that the dome light hadn't come on when he opened the door. Worried that the battery might be dead, he pulled on the headlight knob to see if he was right.

Both beams flared to life. In their glow Bolan spotted a series of pegs on the left-hand wall. Several keys dangled from the pegs.

It took only a few seconds to find one labeled "Pickup." The vehicle purred to life on the first try. Bolan had to jiggle the shift to get the truck into gear, then he was rumbling down the gravel drive to a secondary road, where he turned eastward.

The taillights were long gone. The warrior floored the gas pedal and soon learned the old truck was a workhorse, not a racehorse. The needle pegged at fifty miles an hour and wouldn't go higher no matter how hard he pressed down.

In due course a sign materialized: Hollowcreek 28 Miles. Bolan speculated on whether the terrorists would stop to make a phone call or whether they would keep going until they reached Richmond. His guess would be the call. They needed help fast, somewhere they could lie low until the freighter trip out of the country.

The Executioner had to find a phone himself to inform Brognola of the latest developments. He knew the big Fed would be upset, but the Justice man had been in the business long enough to appreciate the fact that sometimes things fell apart of their own accord and there was nothing anyone could do but pick up the pieces and go on.

The ride seemed to take hours. A pink glow tinted the eastern sky when at last Bolan saw lights ahead. He slowed as he neared Hollowcreek, which was as aptly named a town as the warrior had ever come across. A dozen buildings were situated in a hollow bisected by a bubbling creek. There was a post office, a general store, a number of homes and a diner billed as Ma's Eatery.

Bolan's main interest lay in the phone booth outside the diner. A gray sedan was parked beside it, and a swarthy man was on the phone.

A few hundred feet short of the eatery the warrior slowed and steered to the soft shoulder in front of a dark house. The terrorists were bound to have seen the pickup in the garage. Any closer and they would recognize it and realize he was still alive.

The Executioner shut off the headlights and climbed out on the passenger side. He walked around behind the truck, ducked low and darted across the road into thick undergrowth. Moving parallel to the road, he was soon at the edge of a weed-choked lot. Beyond was the diner.

The terrorist in the booth suddenly slammed down the instrument, then cursed loudly in Arabic. He stalked to the car and leaned down to address the two men inside. A brief consultation resulted in two of the men going into the diner while the third leaned on the front fender of the vehicle to smoke a cigarette.

Slipping into the waist-high weeds, Bolan snaked forward. He had to stop them now. Once they took to the road again, he could never hope to overtake them in the pickup.

A bullfrog croaked, and a dog howled. Combined with the wind rustling the trees, there was enough background noise that Bolan didn't need to be overly concerned about rustling a blade of grass now and then as he closed on his quarry. Or so he thought until he came to the end of the lot and saw his quarry unaccountably walking in his direction.

Bolan went prone and drew his combat knife. He had to dispose of the terrorist silently or risk alerting the hardmen in the diner. He saw the man stop, yawn, then move in a new direction. The man was taking a stroll, nothing more.

Replacing the knife in its sheath, Bolan tucked the M-16 to his shoulder and sighted through the scope. With luck he could drop all three before they got anywhere near the stolen car.

The next moment gunshots thundered in the diner. The terrorist enjoying the smoke appeared as surprised as Bolan. Throwing down the cigarette, he whipped out an autopistol and sprinted toward the door.

A snap judgment was called for. Bolan had to decide whether to nail them on the spot or sit tight in the hope innocent bystanders wouldn't be harmed in the cross fire. A wavering scream determined the issue. He had no choice but to aim squarely between the man's shoulder blades and fire a short burst.

Just then the diner door flew open and the two other terrorists raced out, the huskier of the duo toting a paper bag.

When the Arabs spotted Bolan and their downed companion, they dropped down and scrabbled back inside.

Lights began to go on all over Hollowcreek. Someone shouted a query, demanding to know what was going on.

Surging to his feet, Mack Bolan ran to his left, to a Dumpster. He gained cover as a pistol poked through the diner doorway and cracked several times in swift succession. The bullets spanged harmlessly off the garbage container.

Residents of Hollowcreek were venturing from their homes. Bolan saw a portly man with a shotgun, approaching at a lumbering run. "Go back!" he shouted. "Call the police!"

"What the hell is goin' on, mister?" the man responded. "What's all the shootin' about?"

Bolan wasn't about to disclose that the people responsible for the savage attack on the Capitol were involved. There was no telling how the good people of the hamlet would react. So instead he answered, "The diner is being robbed. Call the police!"

"The diner!" the man roared. "Where's Ma Avery?"

"I don't know."

"Son of a bitch!"

The warrior turned back to the eatery as the man sped off. Bolan hoped the news would spread and keep the residents away long enough for him to circle around and try to find another way in. There had to be a back door. The thought galvanized him into motion. For all he knew, the terrorists were escaping out the back at that very second.

The warrior darted to a metal trash can and from there to the side of the diner. No gunfire greeted him. Racing to the rear corner, he peered cautiously around the edge. There was a back door, but it was closed. He sidled along the wall and grasped the knob. A twist revealed it to be locked.

At last fate was working in Bolan's favor. He had the terrorists cornered. Now all he had to do was keep them pinned down until the cavalry arrived. Brognola would get two live ones after all.

As if to prove the Executioner wrong, a pistol shot rang out at the front of the eatery. The deep boom of a shotgun responded, followed by a smattering of rifle fire and handguns.

Bolan retraced his steps at top speed. The shooting intensified, mingled with the growl of engines and jumbled shouting. He had a fair idea what he would see before he arrived at the front corner, but the reality still jolted him.

The male citizens of Hollowcreek had launched an all-out assault on the eatery. Two pickups and an old sedan, strung out in a row, were shielding a half-dozen or so armed men, just as tanks often shielded infantry in combat. The homegrown militia slowly neared the front of the diner, the men pumping shots into the windows, the door, the walls.

Bolan opened his mouth to warn them away, but a stray slug smacked into the wall and ricocheted, nearly taking his head off in the process. To get out of the line of fire, the warrior spun and raced twenty yards to the north, to a rusted-out hulk of a car. Safe from the firestorm, he squatted and mulled how to put a stop to the fiasco before it was too late.

A moment later the matter was taken out of the warrior's hands. A spectacular explosion literally lifted the small building into the air, the force so powerful it blew out the front of the diner and bowled over several of the onrushing residents. Bolan was buffeted but otherwise unfazed. The walls and roof buckled, collapsing in upon themselves, reducing the eatery to ruins. Flames appeared, licking at the remains.

The warrior blinked, sighed, then turned to sit with his back against the car. When things went wrong, they had a tendency to go wrong in a big way.

"I HEAR they're going to change the name of Hollowcreek to Hole-in-the-Ground."

Seated in a comfortable chair in the den at Stony Man Farm fourteen hours later, Mack Bolan stared across the room at the big Fed but made no comment.

"I'm not blaming you, you understand," Brognola went on wearily. "You couldn't have foreseen all those rounds setting off a gas explosion."

"You're taking this better than I thought you would," Bolan said.

"I'll take that as a compliment."

"I just meant that you've lost your link to the Vulture," the Executioner reminded him.

"Not quite." Brognola held up a sheet of paper. "That name you came up with, Jabal, has paid big dividends. Turns out his full name is Jabal Anaiza. Nationality, Syrian. He has a rap sheet as long as your arm."

"Let me guess. Smuggling?"

"His specialty, you might say. Currently he's employed as chief mate on the freighter *Bolivar*, which is docked at Norfolk."

"Loading or unloading?"

"Unloading farm machinery, according to the manifest. A few hours ago I sent in two agents to check it out. They're due to report anytime." He leaned back and clasped his hands behind his head. "If I read this right, Golden Scimitar planned to hide at the farmhouse until the *Bolivar* was set to lift anchor, then sneak aboard."

Bolan nodded. "They would have been in the clear."

"For a while, anyway. We'd have nailed their butts sooner or later." Brognola tapped the paper. "Now, with them out of the way, we can go after bigger fish."

"You really want this guy, don't you?"

"Can you blame me?" Brognola rejoined. "The Vulture, as he's known in intelligence circles, would be the catch of the decade. The man supplies more arms to more countries and organizations whose interests are inimical to those of the United States than any ten illegal arms czars combined. If we could put him out of operation, we'd cripple the underground network in the worst way."

"All we have to do is find out who this Vulture is."

"Jabal Anaiza is our best lead to date. Once Fredericks and Williamson report in on the shipment, I'll have them pick Anaiza up."

"I'd like the job," Bolan volunteered.

The big Fed's bushy eyebrows arched. "Why waste your time? My boys can handle a simple job like this."

"Nothing about this business is ever simple. Call your bird dogs off and I'll bring Anaiza in."

Hal Brognola studied the warrior. "Okay. You got it."

NORFOLK, VIRGINIA, was one of the leading ports in the entire United States. With so many ships arriving and departing daily, it was possible for a small coastal freighter like the *Bolivar* to slip in and out without drawing much attention.

It didn't take a genius to deduce that the Vulture relied on such anonymity to funnel arms wherever there were buyers. Mack Bolan stood on a pier near where the freighter was docked and wondered if the owners knew the secret purpose for which their ship was being used.

The flag the cargo ship flew was Honduran, a commonplace occurrence, since Honduras was one of three countries that didn't levy taxes on ships and allowed owners to pay the barest minimum in wages. Businesses looking to heft their profit margins were all too happy to transport their goods on such vessels.

Shoving his hands into the pockets of his pea jacket, Bolan tucked his chin to his chest to ward off the biting wind and strolled along the pier for a closer inspection.

Longshoremen were busy unloading cargo. Bolan watched a boom swing cargo out of the hold, then noticed two crewmen talking by the bow rail. One was a scrawny individual with ratlike features dominated by a nose that would have done justice to Pinocchio. There was no mistaking a face like that. Bolan had seen it only hours earlier in a photo Brognola had shown him. Jabal Anaiza.

Wheeling, Bolan walked slowly away. He didn't want to have Anaiza see him before he made his move.

The ship had been under surveillance by federal agents for more than a day and not once had the Syrian stepped onshore. The consensus was that Anaiza had heard or read a news report detailing the clash between members of Golden Scimitar and an elite federal antiterrorism unit, and now Anaiza was lying low out of fear his connection to the fanatics had been uncovered.

Bolan rapped on the rear window of a sedan parked at a nearby curb. The window hissed down and Hal Brognola nodded.

"Ready if you are, Striker."

"Let's do it."

Twilight shrouded the pier as the warrior made his move. He strolled up the gangplank as casual as could be, halting when a bearded crewman stepped out of the shadows.

"Evening, mister. Do you have business aboard this ship?"

"I'm here to see the chief mate."

"Is that a fact?" The man pointed amidships. "Well, you just go up that first companionway there and his cabin is the third door."

Bolan nodded and did as instructed. He stuck his right hand in his pocket and rapped twice with his left.

"Come."

Lifting the latch, the warrior stepped in swiftly and shut the door behind him. "Jabal Anaiza?"

The man was seated at a small desk, writing in a notebook. He glanced up, his beady eyes narrowing, and demanded, "Who might you be? I don't know you."

"Let me be the first to congratulate you on winning," Bolan said pleasantly while taking a stride nearer.

"What the hell are you talking about?" Anaiza asked suspiciously, his hand creeping toward a drawer at his elbow.

"No one has notified you?" Bolan said glibly, taking yet another step. "You've won lifelong accommodations at one of the finest penal institutions in the U.S."

The chief mate flushed red and yanked on the drawer handle, exposing a Smith & Wesson revolver. He scrambled for the gun, his arm a blur.

But as fast as Anaiza was, the Executioner was faster. Bolan's right hand swept out of his pea jacket with the Beretta palmed. The weapon chugged once.

Drilled through the wrist just as he touched the gun, the Syrian recoiled, clutching his arm. He moved as if about to grab the .357 with his good hand, then glanced at the unwavering Beretta and changed his mind. Hatred contorting his features, he raised his hands to his chest and snarled, "You'll never get off the *Bolivar* alive!"

"You let me worry about that," Bolan said. Advancing, he took the Smith & Wesson and shoved it into his left pocket. Then he gripped the Syrian by the shoulder and shoved him toward the low bunk. "Rest awhile. This won't take long."

Scowling, blood dripping down his arm, the chief mate obeyed. "Think you're so damn smart, don't you? Well, FBI man, you're in for a nasty surprise."

"I'm not FBI," Bolan said as he flipped pages in the notebook.

"What, then? Don't tell me you're CIA?"

"No, I'm the man who's going to shoot you in the other wrist if you don't stop talking."

That shut the Syrian up. Bolan closed the notebook and wedged it under the front of his belt. Keeping one eye on Anaiza, he rifled through the drawers. A small black tablet containing a list of cities, sums of money and names went into his pants pocket.

All the while the chief mate fidgeted, often casting nervous looks at the porthole. When the warrior straightened to leave, Anaiza licked his lips and blurted, "Listen, if we go out there, we're both dead. Call in more men, or we'll never step foot on the pier."

"Don't give yourself a heart attack. Federal agents will be waiting for us at the bottom of the gangplank."

"That will be too late!"

Bolan was uncertain whether to believe the Syrian or not. Anaiza's fear seemed genuine, but the chief mate might only be attempting to rattle him so he'd make a mistake and give Anaiza a chance to jump him. "On your feet."

"Please! In the name of God, listen to me!"

"Stay close to me and nothing will happen to you," Bolan said. He waved the Beretta, then trailed the Syrian to the door. "Open it."

Fingers quaking, Anaiza did, but only a few inches, enough for him to peer out.

The warrior prodded him with the Beretta. "Keep going."

Muttering, the chief mate fearfully slid from his quarters, staying close to the bulkhead.

Bolan checked both directions, saw no cause for alarm, and pushed Anaiza ahead of him. There was no sign of the crewman who had challenged him when he boarded. The man had probably gone on about his own business.

"You don't understand," Anaiza whispered urgently. "The person I work for is very thorough. His operation is covered from every angle."

"So?"

"So I'm not the only one on the ship working for him. There are others."

They were nearing the end of the passage. Bolan touched the Beretta to the Syrian's shoulder and commanded, "Stop." Then he slipped past to survey the deck below. It was empty except for several stacks of crates and a net piled near the starboard bulwark. The gangplank beckoned two hundred feet away. "Enough stalling," Bolan growled. "Lead the way."

"Please. I'll take you to the captain's cabin. You can call for help."

"You're the one who will need help if you don't get in gear," Bolan snapped. Seizing the Syrian by the shirt, he pushed him toward the companionway.

The chief mate stumbled, caught hold of the rail for support and glared. "You filthy—"

Whatever else the man was going to say was lost to posterity when the front of his forehead burst outward in a spray of gore.

Bolan was on his stomach before the body hit the floor. He hadn't heard a shot, so the opposition was also using a suppressor. Wriggling forward until he had a clear field of fire, he searched for targets but found none. Based on where Anaiza had been standing and the angle at which the slug had penetrated, Bolan guessed that the gunner was concealed behind several crates fifty feet off to the left.

Retreating to the bulkhead, the Executioner rose into a crouch. He intended to head aft and work his way around the superstructure, but the moment he rose, a bullet whined off the metal a finger's width over his head. Again he went horizontal and rolled close to the rail in time to see a vague shape dart from sight. Now he had a gunner in front and a gunner to the rear.

And who knew how many more?

3

To a man like Mack Bolan, combat strategy came as naturally as breathing. He didn't agonize over each and every little move he made. He simply adjusted to the circumstances and acted accordingly. So the moment he realized his enemies had him trapped between them, he sprang into action.

A leap took Bolan to the forward companionway. He jumped into space, doubling at the waist to present a smaller target, and saw the gunner behind the crates pop up. The warrior fired in midair, but missed. The shot was enough, though, to drive the gunner back under cover.

Bolan landed lightly and threw himself to the right, toward the bulwark. Whirling and sinking to one knee, he glimpsed a huddled form close to the superstructure. The form rose, an object glinting dully in one hand, and the Executioner drilled two shots into the gunner's chest.

Pivoting, the warrior dashed toward the bow, to a cluster of crates that offered sturdy cover nearer the gangplank. The gunner screened by the other crates appeared to the left of them, his pistol spitting lead.

Only Bolan's speed saved him. A mighty leap carried him up and over the smaller of the crates. He banged his knee as he landed but disregarded the pain to return fire. When his clip ran dry, he ducked down.

Mechanically Bolan extracted the magazine and slapped in a new one. He chambered the first round, then raised his eyes to the top of the crate. The deck was momentarily still.

Suddenly a man showed himself by the railing where the Syrian lay. He crouched and seemed to be examining Anaiza.

Since the Executioner had no idea whether this new arrival was a member of the arms network or an innocent crewman, he held his fire. Moments later the man crept back along the passage. A door clicked open, then closed.

Bolan suspected the man had gone into Anaiza's compartment. Why? Was it someone else after incriminating evidence? Bending, the warrior quickly shrugged out of the pea jacket. Holding it in his left hand, the Beretta in his right, he moved to the end of the crate.

An overhand motion sent the jacket sailing. Any experienced gunner would have held his fire long enough to ascertain what was going down, but the gunner behind the other crates uncurled and put three shots into the jacket while it was falling. In that same span the warrior put three shots into him.

Vaulting the crate, Bolan raced to the companionway and flew up the steps. Anaiza had been flipped onto his back, his pockets turned inside out.

The cabin door yielded to Bolan's shoulder and he slanted to one side, holding the Beretta in a two-handed grip. A tall black man squatted beside a nightstand.

Displaying remarkable reflexes, the hardman seized the warrior by the wrist, pivoted and heaved.

Bolan's feet left the floor. He slammed into the bulkhead so hard that pinpoints of lights swirled before his eyes. The hardman's foot lashed out, jarring the warrior's wrist, which caused him to lose his grip on the Beretta.

The Executioner reached for his ankle, for the stiletto he carried in a snug sheath, but the man was on him in the blink of an eye. A stiff hand slashed at Bolan's throat. He blocked it and drove his fist into the man's stomach. It was like hitting solid steel.

Hissing, the hardman brought up a knee, caught Bolan full in the chest and slammed him back against the wall. Then he clamped both hands on Bolan's throat and squeezed.

The warrior knew better than to attempt to break that viselike hold. His foe had the build of a weight lifter. Instead he arced his palm up and in, raking it across his attacker's nose, shattering cartilage and causing the man to step back.

Leaning for added leverage, Bolan kicked, planting his heel where it would do the most good. The man grunted, tottered, then recovered sufficiently to make a break for the doorway. He was almost out the door when there was a loud thud. His head snapped up, he did an ungainly dance rearward and collapsed on top of the desk, a deep gash in his temple.

Hal Brognola calmly entered, slid a pistol into his shoulder holster and commented, "You sure have a knack for piling up bodies."

"You took long enough."

"You were the one who wanted to do this all by his lonesome," Brognola reminded the warrior. "I got tired of waiting, so we came on board. I've got agents making a sweep of the ship even as we speak." He paused. "I noticed the Syrian bought the farm."

"I did salvage these." Bolan tugged the notebook from under his belt and tossed both it and the black tablet to the big Fed. "They might tell you something."

"I hope so or you went to all this trouble for nothing."

Coming from anyone else, Bolan would have viewed the remark as criticism. But Brognola was simply stating a fact, a fact that disturbed the warrior. Twice now he had tangled with people who had ties to the mysterious Vulture and twice he had been left holding the short end of the stick. He didn't like it.

Brognola had been watching his friend's expression. "Not to worry. If this doesn't pan out, we try another way to nail the Vulture."

Bolan only grunted.

Suddenly there was a commotion outside. Feet stomped on the deck. Someone shouted. Then there was a gunshot, the big boom of a heavy-caliber revolver.

The warrior beat Brognola to the door by a stride. Warily sticking his head out, he saw a thin blond man in a three-piece suit racing down the passage toward them.

"He's one of mine," Brognola said. "Williamson."

The agent slid to a halt. "Sir, it's the captain of this ship. LaFlors. We were questioning him when he took a powder. Fredericks has been shot."

"LaFlors?" Brognola asked.

"Beat us to the gangplank. Weaver was at the bottom, but his gun snagged in his holster and LaFlors knocked him into the water."

"Damn it!" Brognola declared. "Can't anything go right anymore?"

"LaFlors is on foot. Do you want me to go after him?" Williamson inquired.

"Go, go." Brognola gestured impatiently. "He's probably caught a cab by now, but you never know. Just watch your back."

Bolan stepped out the door. "I'll watch it for him."

"Striker, wait—"

The Executioner moved off without waiting to hear the rest. He knew that Brognola would only try to stop him, to persuade him that it was unnecessary to lend a hand. Bolan had to differ. Williamson was a brother in arms, an agent devoted to his country and dedicated to stamping out the same evils that Bolan had pledged his life to defeat.

On the way across the deck the warrior made a short detour to reclaim the pea jacket. He slid it on as he ran.

A soaked, coughing agent was clambering from a ladder onto the pier as Bolan and Williamson descended.

"You okay, Weaver?" Williamson called out.

"Lost my pistol," the other responded testily. "It sank to the bottom." He stared at them. "Where are you going?"

"After the one who nailed you," Williamson replied, slowing to negotiate the end of the gangplank.

"Yeah? Bust the sucker one for me, Eddy!"

Bolan and the young agent sprinted along the pier to a street. With the coming of nightfall most of the activity at the docks and the adjacent area had stopped. The street was quiet, with few pedestrians abroad.

"Which way?" Williamson wondered.

"That way," Bolan said, pointing at a bustling junction several blocks off. Taking the lead, he ran all-out.

Williamson huffed and puffed to keep up but still managed to inquire, "If you don't mind my asking, why this way?"

"All the cars, all the people," Bolan explained. "LaFlors can lose himself in the crowd."

"Should have thought of that myself," Williamson griped in self-reproach.

"Nobody's perfect," Bolan said to put the agent at ease.

Moments later they reached the intersection. Bolan halted and looked right and left. The steady stream of pedestrians was unbroken. No one was running.

"It was too much to hope for," Bolan said. "We should head back."

Williamson nodded and began to turn, his gaze absently roving over the buildings across the street. Without warning he grabbed the warrior's arm and pulled Bolan into the shadows. "It's him. LaFlors!"

"Where?"

"There!" Williamson jabbed a finger at a restaurant on the opposite corner. "In the last booth on the right, sitting so his back is to the window."

Bolan saw an overweight man in a flannel shirt, reading a newspaper. "Are you sure?"

"Yes. He's not wearing his cap or his jacket, but it's the same guy. There's no mistaking someone with a build like his. I'd stake my life on it." Williamson headed for the curb. "If you want, I'll go make a positive ID and we can haul him to the *Bolivar*."

"Not so fast," Bolan said. "I'll go."

"Why you?"

"LaFlors got a good look at you when you were interrogating him, didn't he?"

The young Justice agent frowned. "Yes, he did."

"If he sees you, he'll rabbit. Innocent people might be hurt. You stay put and let me handle this."

"Whatever you say," Williamson said sheepishly.

Inwardly Bolan had his doubts the captain would be sitting there in plain sight. LaFlors should be halfway across the city. Maybe, in an effort to impress him, the young agent was letting his eagerness override his better judgment.

Then Bolan thought of the times he had tried the same ruse. Sometimes the best place to hide *was* in plain sight. That old saw about most people not being able to see something right under their own noses was more true than most knew.

When Bolan was convinced the man in the booth wasn't looking, he blended into the flow of pedestrians. At the corner he hung back so that a half-dozen others flanked the curb, screening him from the restaurant.

The light changed, and Bolan joined those hurrying along the crosswalk. On the far side he deliberately avoided looking at the restaurant and kept walking until he was abreast of the entrance.

Two attractive women were emerging. "Allow me," Bolan said, taking the door and holding it open for them. They smiled sweetly and one gave him a frank appraisal. The warrior entered, walking to a counter that fronted the left-hand wall.

Perched on a stool, Bolan picked up the menu and pretended to study the selections. He shifted, slowly turning the stool so he could see the heavyset man out of the corner of his eye. Sure enough, there was a blue jacket and seaman's cap resting beside him.

"What would you like, handsome?"

Bolan faced the pert waitress. "Just a cup of coffee." Setting down the menu, he leaned an elbow on the edge of the counter and twisted so he could keep LaFlors under surveillance. The captain wasn't overly interested in his newspaper. Every thirty or forty seconds he would glance at the intersection.

The coffee came, and Bolan maintained his surveillance. He knew LaFlors had a revolver and wasn't shy about using it, so he was taking no undue risks when the lives of bystanders were at stake. It would be best, he decided, to confront the captain outside. To that end, Bolan was content to wait for LaFlors to leave.

The man appeared in no hurry. Once he placed the paper on the table and picked up the check, but as he began to slide from the booth a patrol car cruised past. LaFlors took one look and immediately buried his face in the newspaper again.

Fifteen minutes crawled by. Bolan nursed his coffee, then ordered a refill.

The next time he checked his quarry LaFlors was riveted to the window, with good reason. Striding briskly along the crosswalk was Ed Williamson. The captain jumped up and lumbered toward the door, his paper in his left hand, forgetting all about paying for his meal in his rush to escape.

The warrior seized the initiative. Shoving off the stool, he closed swiftly, his hand sliding under the pea jacket to curl around the Beretta. He would have nailed the seaman without any problem had there not been a full-length mirror on the wall next to the door.

LaFlors saw Bolan's reflection and had to have guessed Bolan's intent because he spun, panic etching his pudgy face, and lunged, seizing the pert waitress who was on her way to a booth with an order. She dropped two plates, and at the same time LaFlors let go of the folded newspaper, revealing a Charter Arms Pit Bull, which he jammed against the startled woman's temple and cocked. "Back off or she's dead!"

The Executioner froze. No matter what, he wouldn't endanger an innocent. Several of the female patrons screamed, and a man behind the counter bellowed for someone to call the cops.

Balefully regarding Bolan, LaFlors backed toward the door. The waitress was too terrified to resist, to even speak. She allowed herself to be pulled along, her lips quivering, tears at the corners of her eyes.

"Don't follow me!" LaFlors warned. "I'll blow her away if you do."

Bolan wasn't about to press the issue. There was nothing more dangerous than a scared man with a gun, especially one who had nothing to lose. He let LaFlors reach for the door handle, wishing the waitress would duck and give him a clear shot. One was all he needed.

Just then a new element was added. Williamson appeared on the other side of the glass door, his pistol in his hand but not trained on the captain. "Put that gun down!" he yelled. "You're under arrest."

LaFlors had other ideas. Extending his arm, he fired twice through the glass, which shattered on impact. Williamson was flung to the sidewalk by the slugs, a red stain darkening his chest.

Despite himself, Bolan took a stride and started to draw the Beretta. But he got no farther, because the next instant LaFlors gave the waitress a brutal shove and she hurtled forward, right into Bolan. He caught her by the waist but was unable to check her momentum. Together they tottered backward. By the time Bolan disentangled himself, the freighter captain was outside and racing southward with surprising speed.

The warrior gave chase, pausing for a second over the lifeless body of the dead agent. Williamson's eyes were locked wide in death, staring skyward as if in disbelief. He had paid the supreme price for impatience and carelessness.

With a sense of loss at the waste of a young life, Bolan was off after the captain. He spotted LaFlors a block ahead. Weaving among pedestrians, Bolan rapidly gained.

LaFlors glanced back repeatedly. When it became apparent to him that he couldn't hope to elude his grim pursuer, he looked wildly around, spotted an alley to his right and darted into it.

Bolan was too experienced to silhouette himself in the alley mouth. He stopped at the corner, crouched and took a peek. Inky shadows shrouded the interior, preventing him from seeing more than five or six feet with any clarity. Boxes and trash cans lined the walls, and litter was everywhere.

A tin can rattled deep in the alley. The moment it did, Bolan raced along the inner wall until he came to a trash can. He probed the dark depths but saw no one. Silence fell again, and after a minute the warrior catfooted forward, the Beretta in hand.

Moments later Bolan spotted a high brick wall at the end of the alley, too high for a heavy man like LaFlors to scale without a ladder. The captain had outsmarted himself and was trapped, which made him doubly dangerous.

Creeping from cover to cover, the warrior traveled scores of feet until he reached a huge pile of cardboard boxes that barred his path. He edged around them, bent at the knees, avoiding cans scattered on the ground. The sight of them made him think of the rattling he had heard earlier, and as he turned to give the boxes a closer scrutiny they exploded outward and a great bulk reared above him.

The captain leveled his pistol, firing a hasty shot that missed. Bolan leveled the Beretta and snapped off a shot of his own just as the desperate captain plowed into him. They both crashed to the ground among the litter, LaFlors with a brawny hand clamped on Bolan's wrist, Bolan with a hand clamped on the captain's wrist. Neither could bring his gun to bear unless he broke free.

Under ordinary circumstances the Executioner would have made short work of a man like LaFlors. Bolan was in prime physical condition; LaFlors weighed a hundred pounds more than he should have, and little of it was muscle. But the captain was on top, pinning Bolan flat. Unable to use his legs, the warrior strained mightily in an effort to heave LaFlors to one side. It was like trying to heave a massive lump of clay. The best Bolan could do was lift his adversary a few inches.

Sneering, LaFlors struggled to force his pistol nearer to Bolan's head. Simultaneously he tried to ram his knee into the warrior's groin. The Executioner felt the captain's leg move and shifted enough to deflect the blow with his thigh.

He put all of his strength into shoving LaFlors off, but couldn't. Frustrated, he suddenly changed his tactics and pulled the captain toward him. As the man's face swooped down, Bolan bunched his neck muscles and rammed his forehead into the captain's nose.

The head butt had the desired effect. LaFlors cried out as his nostrils were crushed, then jerked back.

Able to move his legs at last, Bolan tucked them to his chest and lashed out, his feet hitting his adversary in the stomach, tumbling him into the boxes. Bolan pushed upright, took a step and rapped the Beretta against the captain's skull. The man went limp.

"Took you long enough."

Bolan whirled at the first syllable, then slowly relaxed.

Brognola walked up and nudged LaFlors with a toe. "Well, finally something has gone our way. Between what I expect him to tell us and what we'll uncover on the *Bolivar,* I imagine it won't be long before you tackle the Vulture himself."

The Executioner thought of the slain senators, Ed Williamson and the riddled elderly farm couple. "I can hardly wait."

4

"Ladies and gentlemen, this is your captain speaking. Welcome aboard Flight 109 nonstop from Miami to Rio de Janeiro. You may now remove your seat restraints."

The captain went on, talking about the duration of the flight and certain safety rules, but Mack Bolan had heard the information so many times that he shut out the rest, leaned his seat back at a more comfortable angle and rested his head close to the window so he could enjoy the magnificent view.

Rio de Janeiro, Bolan reflected, the next rung on the ladder that would bring him to the Vulture. He hoped the intel Brognola had turned up proved worthwhile and he wasn't wasting time following up a dead end.

Lulled by the soft cushions and the expanse of sky and sea below, Bolan found himself starting to doze. Shrugging, he sat up. His time would be better spent in reviewing all they knew, if only to see if there was anything they had overlooked. On the face of things, though, it seemed pat enough.

LaFlors had been a tough nut to crack but had finally opened up. He'd confessed to accepting payoffs from Jabal Anaiza to look the other way when unauthorized shipments were delivered or unloaded. According to him, there had been three other members of the Vulture's organization on board—the two Bolan killed and the black taken into custody by the federal agents.

Jamal Burundi was the third man's name. He had been working under Anaiza only a few months. When he'd found the Syrian dead, he'd gone into the chief mate's cabin to retrieve the man's notebook, confident he would be well rewarded by Anaiza's superior for keeping it safe.

The notebook, however, contained little information that wasn't on the ship's manifests. It was the black tablet that proved a gold mine of valuable details concerning the illicit arms network. From it the Justice Department learned the names, addresses and phone numbers of operatives and officials who were on the take. They could bring the organization to its knees, if they wanted. But they still hadn't uncovered the Vulture's identity.

Based on the pattern of distribution, it was believed that the arms czar operated out of Rio de Janeiro. One particular name in the notebook cropped up again and again, leading them to conclude it was the man Anaiza had taken orders from.

Bolan was on his way to contact that man, and he hoped it would lead to a meet with the Vulture. The plan Brognola had cooked up called for him to pose as a member of Golden Scimitar.

"It should be a breeze," Brognola had said during their meeting. "His father was Iraqi, his mother Italian. You look enough like him to fool anyone who hasn't actually met him."

"But the word has already gone out that every member of the band died," Bolan had noted. "It's been in all the papers and newscasts."

"We've just issued a new press release." He'd picked up the item and read an excerpt. "'After sifting through the debris, the government now believes one terrorist is unaccounted for and all law-enforcement agencies have been directed to make his apprehension their first priority.'"

"What's his name?" Bolan had asked.

"Yusuf Atasi. He used the alias Tony Bianco."

AT MIAMI INTERNATIONAL Airport, a dark-haired man who walked with a limp entered a phone booth and dialed the overseas operator. When she came on the line and requested his routing code, he replied, "Twenty-one."

"Rio de Janeiro. The number you wish to call?"

The man told her, added he was calling collect and gave her his name. Moments later another man came on the line.

"You should know better than to call here."

"I have nowhere else to turn," said the man in Miami.

"What do you want?"

"I need money. A new passport. A ticket out of the country."

The man in Rio sighed. "All that can be arranged. But I must tell you that my employer is most displeased. You are aware of what happened to Jabal?"

"Yes."

"He is not easily replaced."

"That wasn't my doing."

"Then how did they learn of his connection to you?"

"I don't know."

"Hold on a minute," the man in Rio told him. There was silence at his end for a long time, then, "Very well.

In four hours go to the Cloverleaf Motel. Ask for Enrico. He will arrange for you to obtain the items you have requested.''

"What should I do until then?"

"Do whatever you wish. Just be at the motel at the designated time. My employer is very eager to have a talk with you."

"Tell him I have nothing to hide."

"I hope so, for your sake Senhor Atasi."

MACK BOLAN BREEZED through customs and carried his suitcase to the front of the terminal. He had no sooner stepped to the curb than a taxi braked beside him. The driver fell all over himself opening the door for Bolan and taking his suitcase.

In minutes they were headed into the second-largest city in Brazil, traveling along tree-lined, winding roads. The driver knew a little English and proudly pointed out landmarks such as Sugarloaf Mountain and Maracana Stadium. While the driver rambled on, Bolan made certain to check for a tail. As near as he could tell, there was none.

The warrior made only one comment during the long drive. He had noticed that the buildings and streets were being decorated with gaily colored lights and ribbons, so he asked why.

"Surely you joke, *senhor*," the driver replied. "Tomorrow night is the first night of our carnival!"

With all Bolan had on his mind, he had completely forgotten about Rio's most famous annual event.

"That is why you are here, yes?" the driver asked.

"I wouldn't miss it for the world."

The driver chortled. "I knew it! I knew you were—how do you say?—pulling my foot?"

A room had been booked for the warrior at the Hotel Elegancia. He took the elevator to the third floor, opened the door and tensed at the sight of an elderly Brazilian seated in a plush chair. Then he recognized the intruder and smiled.

"Welcome to Rio, Mr. Belasko."

"It's Bianco this time around," Bolan said as he entered the room and tossed his suitcase onto another chair. "How have you been, João?" he asked, offering his hand.

João Peixoto, an old acquaintance of both Bolan and Brognola, smiled. "I have added more gray hairs since I saw you last, Senhor Bianco. Working at the ministerio does that to a person. Too many long hours, too many headaches like the one you have come to cure."

"I'm supposed to relay Hal's regards."

"I trust time has treated him well?" Peixoto inquired. "I still fondly remember the old days when he would drink me under the table. How that man could down so much whiskey and still stay on his feet, I will never know."

"Learn something every day," Bolan said, grinning.

"*Senhor?*"

"Were you able to get your hands on everything I requested?"

"You can't be serious? Find a Desert Eagle in Rio? A howitzer would have been easier." Peixoto rose and walked to the sofa where a duffel bag had been placed. He worked the zipper and began to remove hardware. "I did the best I could. You should like this Para-Ordnance forty-five." He tossed the pistol to Bolan and pulled out two more, one much smaller than the other. "For extra measure I threw in a 9 mm Tanarmi. And since no one in our line of work should go anywhere without an ace in the hole, I added this Targa twenty-two.''

Bolan doubted he would find any use for such a low-caliber firearm, but he kept silent. "What else?"

"I think you will be pleasantly surprised." Peixoto put down the pistols and held up two submachine guns. "I know you have used a mini-Uzi before. This one comes complete with a suppressor." He wagged the other subgun. "And this is an INA M-953, which, as you might know, has proved quite popular with our state police forces."

"How about something for long range?"

"There I have outdone myself." The Brazilian added the Uzi and the INA to the pile and reached into the duffel with both hands. "A Weatherby was out of the question. Instead I found a Whitworth Express."

The rifle gleamed in the sunlight. Bolan walked over and took it into his hands, admiring the craftsmanship. The Whitworth was every bit as reliable as the Weatherby, and in the hands of an expert marksman was capable of dead-center accuracy at distances of three hundred yards or more. "What about ammo?" he asked.

"I have a .458 Winchester. I trust this is enough stopping power, even for you?"

"I could drop a rogue elephant."

"Or a vulture, eh?"

"You were right. You have outdone yourself," Bolan said, admiring his little arsenal.

The Brazilian gave the duffel a whack. "There is enough ammunition to fight off an army. Plus some extras I thought you might need."

The Executioner opened the duffel wide. In addition to fifteen boxes of various ammo, at least two spare magazines for each of the submachine guns and extra clips and holsters for the pistols, there were grenades, Thunder Strips and four pounds of C-4 plastic explosive. He also had his choice from seven different knives. "What did you do? Rob an armory?"

"I did something better. The irony appealed to me."

"How so?"

"All of this ordnance," Peixoto said, gesturing, "was taken from vermin who worked for the Vulture."

"I'll be sure to send him a thank-you note." Bolan removed his jacket and picked up a suitable shoulder holster for the Para-Ordnance. "Now, let's get down to business. What can you tell me about the man I came here to contact?"

"Roberto Garza is not unknown to us. Some years ago he was arrested for carrying a concealed weapon and later for selling a stolen gun to an undercover officer." He reclaimed his chair. "Strictly small-time. And after those two arrests, there was nothing. To be frank, I never would have suspected him of having ties to the Vulture. Apparently Garza has climbed in the underworld ranks."

"The address Hal's people found in the tablet?"

"Is that of a small apartment on the north side of the city. A very run-down neighborhood. Not exactly a slum, but the worst element fraternize there."

"Perfect for a man like Garza."

"But not his true residence, from the look of things," Peixoto speculated. "Those two arrests early in his career must have made him a very circumspect person for him to have eluded detection all this time."

"Have you had it under surveillance?" Bolan asked as he strapped a sheath for a combat knife to his right ankle.

"From the moment my old friend contacted me. Garza arrives each morning at seven, stays until noon, leaves for two hours, then comes back and doesn't leave again until seven or eight. Oddly he has had very few visitors. We have tried tailing him after he departs, but he is too watchful, too slippery."

"Phone calls?"

Peixoto frowned. "The request for a tap was somehow lost in the paperwork shuffle for a day, so we did not get approval until shortly before I left to pick you up at the airport. Within the hour we will be recording all his incoming and outgoing calls."

"Maybe we'll get lucky." Bolan began replacing the hardware in the bag. He picked up the Targa, held it in his palm a moment, then decided to strap it to the small of his back.

"I would not get my hopes up, were I you," Peixoto commented. "The Vulture never makes mistakes."

"Never?"

"Absolutely never. We would have nailed him long before this if he had slipped up just once. He is an enigma, my friend, and unspeakably vicious."

"You must know something about him."

"I have a few suspicions, nothing more, based on obvious deductions. For instance, he must be extremely wealthy. As we both know, with great wealth comes great power."

"Meaning he has important political and military connections."

"That would be my guess. He would need influence in high places to hide his operation so effectively. I would not put it past him to have a senator and a general or two in his pocket. Perhaps a couple of judges, too."

Bolan didn't like that particular news one bit. A run-of-the-mill arms dealer was hard enough to bring down. Security was always tight, and usually there were countless gunners who had to be dealt with in order to reach the top man.

But a criminal such as the Vulture was in a whole different class. To get at him Bolan would have to penetrate layer after layer of protection. He'd have to contend not only with an army of hardmen, but also with possible interference from those the Vulture had bought. If he wasn't careful, he might find himself thrown into a prison somewhere and left there to rot.

"Are you ready?" Peixoto asked.

The warrior zipped the duffel. "As ready as I'll ever be."

AN HOUR LATER the warrior paused outside the door to Roberto Garza's apartment and loosened the Para-Ordnance in its rig. This was the moment of truth. He hoped that Justice's string of assumptions were right— that Yusuf Atasi's sole access to the arms network had been through Jabal Anaiza, that Atasi had never met Garza, never been to Rio. If the Feds were wrong, he'd find himself weathering a hailstorm of lead.

It was a risk Bolan had to take. In the high-stakes game of life and death in which he willingly took part, no one could predict the roll of the dice. He never knew when his life would be on the line, but the uncertainty didn't cause him to shirk his duty to his country or abandon the principles he held so dear.

The warrior rapped twice. Moments later the door was yanked wide by a bulldog of a Brazilian who sported a thin mustache.

"Yes?" the man asked in Portuguese.

"Roberto Garza?" Bolan asked, although he already knew it was from surveillance photos João had shown him.

"Who wants to know?" Garza demanded in his own language.

"Yusuf Atasi," Bolan responded. *"Fala Ingles?"* He switched to English. "I'm afraid my Portuguese is not all that good."

Garza appeared dumbfounded for a few seconds. "Yes, I speak English," he blurted, studying Bolan. "And yes, I am the one you seek." Leaning out, he looked both ways, gripped Bolan's arm, pulled him into the room and shut the door. "I know who you are. But what are you doing here? Have you no brains?"

"I had nowhere else to go," Bolan said. "The rest were all killed. Even Jabal."

"Tell me something I don't know," Garza responded, a suspicious glint coming into his dark eyes. "How is it you were able to escape?"

"It was the will of God. I went to buy gasoline for the car and when I drove back, the farmhouse had been destroyed and the area was swarming with federal agents. I barely got out of there without being caught."

"You were most fortunate."

"Since then I have been on the run," Bolan continued, using the story concocted by Brognola. "I remembered Jabal mentioning you, and since I had nowhere else to turn, here I am."

"How did you find me?"

Bolan forced a friendly grin. "With men in our profession, there is always a way."

Garza nodded. "True enough, I suppose. Come with me. I would hear the whole story so that I can make a full report." He escorted the warrior into a sparsely furnished living room. "This place leaves much to be desired, but then, I only work here." Garza laughed at his lame joke.

"Will your boss be by later?" Bolan probed.

Garza abruptly became stern. "His comings and goings are of no concern to you. He does as he wants, when he wants. If he decides it is in his best interest to see you, he will arrange a meet through me."

"I was just curious."

"Let me give you some advice. Those who last the longest in our organization are those who show the least amount of curiosity about matters that do not rightfully concern them. Understand?"

"I never make the same mistake twice."

"Good." Garza indicated a chair. "Now tell me everything."

For the next half hour Bolan fed Garza a phony story about the raid on the Capitol and its aftermath that included enough genuine details to be believable.

"So you were not at Hollowcreek at all?" Garza inquired at the conclusion.

"No," Bolan answered.

"Where did you hide? How did you sneak out of the country?"

"I have friends," Bolan said. "Friends who would rather not be mentioned by name."

"I do not ask for myself."

"If your boss wants to know, he can ask me personally. Him I'll tell everything." The Executioner let a note of irritation creep into his voice. "I didn't go to all the trouble I did to get here just to spend all my time answering questions from one of his lieutenants."

Garza reddened. "You don't trust me, Senhor Atasi?"

"I didn't say that. It's a matter of getting what I want, and the only way to do that is to go straight to the top."

"And what exactly *do* you want?"

"To work for him in whatever capacity he will let me."

"You would abandon your noble cause of wiping out the capitalist pigs of this world?" Garza's voice dripped sarcasm.

"A man has to be a realist," Bolan replied. "I had plenty of time to think after my friends were killed." He paused to choose his next words carefully. They had to be believable or he would never be permitted to meet the Vulture. "Those senators we killed, what good did it do? They will soon be replaced, and the new senators will carry on the imperialist goals of their predecessors. So we accomplished nothing by our attack, except to garner a few sensational headlines. No, I could do more good by joining your organization and helping arm those throughout the world who believe in the same cause."

"How interesting," Garza said. "I will be certain to relay your sentiments."

"I would be in your debt if you could set up a face-to-face. I wouldn't take much of his time. I promise."

"I will see what I can do."

It occurred to Bolan that not once during their conversation had Garza referred to the Vulture by name or even an initial. There hadn't been the faintest clue to the Vulture's identity. If nothing else, the arms czar hired underlings who knew how to keep their mouths shut.

"Until then, is there anything you need? Money perhaps?"

"I could use some," Bolan admitted.

Garza left the room, returning shortly with a wad of bills a quarter of an inch thick. "This should serve for a while. Anything else? A place to stay?"

"I don't have one yet."

"We must rectify that." Again the Brazilian left the room. This time he brought back a slip of paper bearing an address. "You will go there and ask for Phillipe. He rents rooms at the back of his house. I will call to let him know you are coming."

"Thanks."

"When I want to see you, I will leave a message with him."

Bolan stood. "I hope I won't have to wait long."

"Not long at all. I assure you."

The Brazilian led the way to the door and held it open. "It goes without saying that you must not have any trouble with the police. Not getting drunk and making a spectacle of yourself in public. No beating up whores."

"I'll be on my best behavior."

"I'm sure you will," Garza replied suavely.

Stuffing the wad in his pocket, Bolan started to leave.

"One last thing," the lieutenant said, almost as an afterthought. "I forgot to ask if you are armed."

"I have a knife."

"That is all?"

"I couldn't very well smuggle a gun into the country."

"It is not very smart for those in our line of work to go around without the means to protect themselves. You will need a pistol. I will have one for you the next time we meet."

"Hope I can repay you for all you've done."

An odd grin curled Garza's lips. "Don't worry in that respect. I'm sure I will think of a way."

5

Mack Bolan was a man of action. When he had a problem, he faced it head-on. When in a fight for his life, he went for the throat. When a drug lord or a Mafia don or an arms dealer needed to be taken down, he preferred the direct approach.

So this business of infiltrating the Vulture's network by posing as Yusuf Atasi didn't sit well with him. He'd rather have his quarry at the end of his sights than be playing a devious battle of wits.

Now, having made the opening move in his bid to topple the Vulture, Bolan wasn't pleased by the outcome. Although Garza had bent over backward to help him out, he had a nagging suspicion that there was more to the lieutenant's actions than had met the eye. The troubling aspect was that Bolan couldn't put his finger on the reason he felt as he did.

During the taxi ride to the address Garza had provided, Bolan reviewed the meeting in his mind again and again. He hadn't come to any set conclusions when he arrived at his destination in a section of Rio tourists never saw.

The streets were narrow and dark. The grimy houses were packed close together. Prostitutes and flinty-eyed men roamed in search of easy marks.

The particular house Bolan sought was located adjacent to a noisy bar. He paid off the driver, aware of being scrutinized by several young toughs loitering outside. His knock on the door was answered by a rail of a man whose mouth was locked in a perpetual scowl. "I was told to ask for Phillipe," the warrior said when the man simply stood there.

"I had a call. Your room is ready."

A dingy hall brought them to a short flight of stairs. Bolan's room was at the top, little more than a cubicle that reeked of sweat and other unpleasant odors.

"One hundred a week," Phillipe declared, holding out a palm. "In advance."

Bolan counted out the money.

"I do not provide meals. If you want to eat, visit the bar. They serve food from ten in the morning until midnight." Phillipe took the money and began to count it himself. "I do not provide towels or soap. You must provide your own. I do not allow women on the premises. If you are caught, I will throw you out. Nor do I allow drunks."

"A regular country club," Bolan said.

"Senhor?"

"Do you have a telephone if I should need one?"

"No. There is a public phone four blocks west of here."

"Only four?"

Once Bolan was alone, he checked for electronic bugs. There were none in the obvious hiding places, but he had learned a long time ago not to rely on the obvious. Not that he would say anything incriminating in that room anyway.

After ten minutes Bolan left. Earlier he had agreed to meet João Peixoto at the Hotel Elegancia at eight that evening, which gave him time for a quick bite. The young hoodlums were still near the door, and they gave him the same sort of collective look as would a pack of hungry wolves.

No one seemed the least interested in Bolan once he was inside. He took a corner table where he could keep an eye on the door and ordered black beans with bits of pork and beef.

A scruffy tough entered when Bolan was halfway through his meal. The man went to the bar and stood so he could see the warrior's table in the mirror. Bolan pretended not to notice. He paid the bill and walked out to find the youths were gone.

Dusk claimed Rio. The shadows had lengthened, and there were fewer people moving about. That would change when Rio's night life rolled into full swing, in about one hour.

Bolan listened to the dull echo of his own footsteps as he headed westward. He had gone a block when other footsteps sounded to the rear. A furtive glance showed he had a tail—the scruffy tough.

A six-story building stood in front of Bolan. The shadows at its base were darker than elsewhere, so it was there the warrior expected to be jumped.

They came at him from out of recessed doorways and around corners, armed either with knives or pipes or in one case a length of chain. There was no escaping without going through them.

Bolan ducked under the knife swing of the first gang member to reach him and broke the man's knee with a well-placed kick. The second man carried a piece of pipe that he drove at Bolan's skull. The warrior twisted, the pipe missing. Bolan delivered a roundhouse to the jaw that left the tough sprawled in the street.

Five more remained. They learned from the fates of their rash companions and slowed to circle Bolan. The street was temporarily deserted. If anyone watched from an upper-story window, they were keeping out of sight.

Another knife wielder charged. Again Bolan dropped under the streaking blade, but this time he grasped the hilt of the combat knife strapped to his ankle. As he rose he plunged the blade into his attacker's chest. Screeching, the man flung himself backward, then collapsed.

Suddenly a burly brute produced a gun. Bolan had no more than glimpsed the glint of the barrel than he whirled and tossed the knife in a smooth overhand throw. The blade sank to the hilt in the hardman's throat, and he lost all interest in shooting the warrior. Instead, he staggered down a short flight of steps and sank limply against a door.

The three remaining punks charged all at once. Bolan dissuaded one with a snap kick to the groin. Then the last two were on him. A pipe glanced off Bolan's temple, stunning him long enough for the second man to grab him from behind and try to stab him in the side of his throat.

Bolan brought up an arm, blocking the man's wrist. At the same time he drove his other elbow into the tough's stomach. Before he could follow through, the guy with the club lashed out again. The Executioner had to tuck an ear to a shoulder to keep from having his head pulped.

Snapping forward, Bolan grasped the arm that looped his neck and heaved, throwing the gang member behind him into the one in front. Both toppled to the ground, and Bolan made a stab for the Para-Ordnance, but as he was snatching it loose a third hardman hurtled out of nowhere and tackled him. The collision knocked the pistol from his hand.

Bolan smashed an elbow into the tackler's face, causing the man to rear back. Momentarily free, the warrior bent and grabbed the Targa. His first shot caught the knife-wielding young man between the eyes. His second shot drilled into the chest of the guy with the pipe. Then, shifting, he fired twice and took out the tackler as the man brought up a switchblade.

Only one gang member remained on his feet. The one with the shattered kneecap was heading northward at what could only be described as a rapid limp.

Bolan allowed the man to live. The .22 wasn't loud, but the shots were bound to have been heard, and he had to head out before the police arrived. Retrieving the Para-Ordnance and the combat knife, he hastened to the west and found a cab just as a siren howled in the distance. A speeding police car passed the cab a minute later.

At the Elegancia Bolan took a shower and changed into fresh clothes. He cleaned the Targa and was in the act of filling the clips when Peixoto arrived.

"So how did the meet go?"

Bolan detailed his visit, then told about the run-in with the young toughs.

"*Porcos!*" the Brazilian snapped in disgust. "Such gangs are a scourge! In certain sections of the city they infest the streets as rats do the sewers. They rob people in broad daylight and often rape and kill. The police try their best, but there is only so much they can do."

"Shades of L.A.," the warrior remarked.

"I will inquire into the police investigation, discreetly of course, and insure that they do not interfere with our operation."

Just then the telephone rang. Bolan answered and handed the receiver to his contact. Peixoto became excited at whatever was being imparted, and when he hung up he beamed.

"Some luck at last! Garza has broken his usual routine. My men have been able to follow him to a villa outside the city. From a distance they have seen guards patrolling the grounds."

"Garza's residence, you think?"

"Perhaps the Vulture's. My men report that when Garza arrived at the gate, the guards had him get out so they could frisk him and search his vehicle. They would hardly have done so if the villa is his." He smacked his right fist into his left palm. "We might have the Vulture at last!"

"Would the Vulture have one of his top lieutenants frisked?" Bolan asked skeptically.

"According to what little we have learned of him, he is just the type. Paranoid as can be. Trusts no one, takes no chances."

"So what now?"

"We will go have a look for ourselves," Peixoto proposed. "This could be the break we have been waiting for."

THE RIDE TOOK nearly three hours. At the top of a hill the Brazilian turned onto a dirt road. After traveling a quarter of a mile, he parked at the side of the road behind a green sedan. Two men got out and guided Peixoto and Bolan through thick trees to a spot overlooking a verdant valley.

The villa lay below, bathed in floodlights. Covering more than four acres, it resembled a fortress more than it did a country dwelling. High walls enclosed a half-dozen buildings, five of which were built like bunkers. The sixth was a large house.

Bolan counted two guards at the wrought-iron gate, two more roving the grounds. Four cars stood in the driveway, a truck near one of the bunkers. "Is Garza still there?" he inquired.

Peixoto had been talking in hushed tones to his men. He nodded and said, "The black Mercedes is his. I say we go in now, while they're all there."

"Rushing things, aren't we?"

"Can you blame me? You know how long we have been after this bastard. If we wait, he might fly the coop, as you Americans say." Peixoto gestured angrily at the villa. "Do you realize how many lives have been snuffed out because of the Vulture? Not directly, of course, but indirectly, by the fanatics he supplies with arms? In all the years I have been trying to bring him down, this is the closest I have come. I cannot permit the opportunity to pass."

"What do you have in mind?"

"Simple. We go in fast and hard and take down everyone we find."

Bolan was studying the walls. He spied a wooden door in the north wall and noticed that the roof of one of the bunkers was within leaping distance of the south wall. Pointing them out, he said, "We don't have enough men. If we go barging in there, the Vulture could easily slip out before we nail him. Either you radio for backup—"

"It would take too long."

"Or we do it my way," Bolan finished.

"You have a plan?"

"Such as it is." The warrior didn't like being rushed into a confrontation, but he didn't see where he had any choice. He'd promised Brognola that he would cooperate with Peixoto in order not to ruffle any political feathers. More important, if the men failed to bag the Vulture, the weapons dealer would go so far underground no one would ever find him again. So he had to help, whether he liked it or not.

"I bow to your experience in these matters," Peixoto was saying. "How should we proceed?"

"In order to insure the Vulture doesn't escape, we have to bottle up the villa. You cover the south wall, have your men cover the west and east walls. If anyone tries to get past you, stop them."

"And you?"

"I'll go in through the main gate."

"All by yourself?"

Bolan's mouth curved upward. "Just me and my calling cards." He turned to go but paused when he spied a figure walk out of the house and head for the Mercedes. Even at that distance he recognized Roberto Garza.

"Damn! He is leaving!" Peixoto said.

"We can cut him off," Bolan suggested.

"I would rather not. What if the people at the villa hear shots or a crash? Or what if he has a cellular phone and is able to use it before we intercept him? No, let's allow him to go back to Rio. We can always pick him up later."

Once again Bolan was reminded of why he would rather work alone. "It's your show," he said as they hurried to the cars.

The warrior took out the duffel and opened it on the ground. He slung the mini-Uzi over his left arm and the INA subgun over his right. Spare magazines for both went into his pockets, as did several grenades.

Peixoto and his men produced three INAs from the trunk of the other car.

Once they were ready Bolan assumed the lead, driving over the crest and down a gradual slope until they were in undergrowth that bordered the serpentine road. The warrior stopped and watched the Mercedes climb toward them. It bothered him to let Garza slip away, but he bowed to Peixoto's wishes and did nothing as the car sped past.

The tangle of vegetation permitted them to approach close to the high walls without being detected. Bolan was surprised that a man as careful as the Vulture hadn't thought to clear the land for an acre or two around the villa. He received another surprise when he was close enough to see the two guards clearly and discovered they were carrying pump-action shotguns, not assault rifles or submachine guns.

The warrior wondered if the Vulture's reputation was vastly overblown. With all the hardware the arms czar had at his disposal, he chose to arm his personal guards with shotguns. It was unbelievable.

"Give us ten minutes to get into position," Peixoto whispered.

The warrior nodded and settled down to wait. He examined the walls for surveillance cameras or other security devices but saw none.

Both guards leaned against the wall, smoking and talking. Both had their shotguns slung. They gave every indication of being rank amateurs, not the highly skilled hardmen Bolan had expected a man like the Vulture would employ.

A vague feeling of uneasiness swept over Bolan, a feeling that all was not as it should be. Nothing about the setup rang true, and the more he thought about it, the more convinced he became that they should pull back and reconsider. But Peixoto and the others would soon be in place. He was committed. There was no turning back.

The ten minutes were soon over. Bolan adjusted the INA so that it rode behind his back, freeing both hands for the mini-Uzi. Advancing warily, he reached a thick bush twenty feet from the gate.

One of the guards threw his cigarette to the ground and turned in Bolan's direction, unslinging his weapon. The warrior rose from cover and cut loose, stitching slugs across the chests of both gunners. Wordlessly they dropped in a heap of tangled limbs.

Bolan raced to the gate, surprised that there were no locks, no high-tech electronic equipment to warn of intruders. A bolt had to be thrown, then Bolan was inside with his back to the left-hand wall.

The warrior sprinted toward the house. As he gained the garden path that led to the veranda, a German shepherd dog hurtled out of the bushes, snarling and snapping in a frenzy. Bolan threw himself to the side, narrowly evading the dog. He spun to confront the animal and saw it do an ungainly flip as it fell back at the end of a glittering chain. The dog yipped in pain, and answering barks erupted in the house.

Men started to shout, both in the house and in one of the bunkers. Moments later more floodlights flared to life.

Speed was everything now. Bolan pulled out a grenade, ran close to a window at the corner of the house and heaved the bomb through the pane. Doing an about-face, he sprinted to get out of the blast radius, taking ten strides and throwing himself to the earth a fraction of a second before the detonation.

The blast blew out several windows, a door and part of a wall.

As Bolan got to his feet the turf around him erupted in miniature geysers. Twisting, he saw three hardmen bearing down on him from the far corner of the house. He flattened one with the Uzi, which then ran dry. Going prone, he switched to the INA, firing short, controlled bursts to conserve his ammo. The two remaining hardmen dropped to the ground.

Lights blazed to life all through the house. Bolan slapped a fresh magazine into the Uzi while listening to a confused jumble of shouting and colorful oaths.

A few swift strides took Bolan to the veranda. The smoke was so thick he couldn't see more than a yard in front of his face, which suited his needs. Plunging through the ragged gap in the wall he abruptly came nose to nose with a shocked gunner. The man's eyes were filled with tears, and he wheezed uncontrollably. Bolan flicked a foot into the gunner's groin, and as the man doubled over, the warrior rapped the butt of the subgun against the guy's temple.

Someone upstairs was bellowing orders. Bolan let the yells lead him up a flight of stairs to a sparsely furnished hallway. He could see seven doors, four on the left, three on the right. One of the doors opened and out walked a bare-chested man carrying a carbine. He was rubbing sleep from his eyes when he should have been wide awake, a mistake he paid for when Bolan sent him to meet his Maker.

Quickly the warrior stood and advanced. The first two doors were open, the rooms empty. The next contained an elderly woman still in bed, her features distorted in stark terror. She screeched when Bolan appeared, and ducked under the covers as if to shield herself from a hail of bullets.

Bolan didn't stop. He checked all the rooms but one. To the south gunfire broke out, the chatter of an Uzi punctuated by pistol fire. Someone trying to flee had run into João Peixoto.

From the last room came a sharp rasping sound, as if a window were being thrown open. Bolan ran to the doorway in time to glimpse a dark-haired man wearing only underwear leap from a sill. He dashed across the room and dropped to one knee. The man was scrambling down a tree with the agility of a monkey. Bolan brought the Uzi to bear, but the man was on the other side of the tree and he couldn't get a clear shot.

The warrior was about to go out the window in pursuit when footsteps in the hall heralded the arrival of reinforcements. Pivoting on a heel, he squeezed off three rounds as a man holding a rifle barreled into the room. Slugs cored the gunner's torso, flinging him back into the hallway.

Bolan bent low, eased out the window and leaped to the tree. The man he was chasing was almost to the northwest corner of the house. Climbing down would take too long, so Bolan dropped to the ground and winced as he twisted his ankle slightly. Ignoring the pain, he aimed the Uzi just as the fleeing figure sped from sight.

The warrior broke into a run. Something told him that the man he was after might be the king of the heap, none other than the Vulture himself. Bolan couldn't let him get away. He took the corner on the fly, but his quarry was nowhere to be seen. Racing toward the front of the house, he heard a noise that lent wings to his feet; someone was starting a car.

The Vulture was about to escape, and there was no one at the front gate to stop him.

6

The Executioner reached the front corner and saw the car roaring down the drive. He cut loose with the Uzi, switching to the INA when the clip ran dry. He unleashed a burst that ripped into the trunk and the rear tires.

The car swerved as the traction went, and the driver lost control. The vehicle careened into a tree, barely jarring to a stop before the man behind the wheel leaped out and ran for the open gate.

It was a long shot. Bolan wedged the stock to his shoulder, took deliberate aim, then fired. The first rounds were short, kicking up dirt at the man's heels, so Bolan compensated. A patchwork of red dots blossomed on the man's back, punching him into the dirt.

Bolan scanned the yard and the house. The villa was quiet except for the fierce barking of the German shepherd.

The big man jogged to the first bunker, kicked in the door and went in low and primed for trouble. Scattered about were uneven stacks of crates. He walked slowly among them, noting words stenciled in block letters here and there. There was armament of every sort—SMGs, grenades, rocket launchers, bazookas, ammunition.

A complete sweep failed to turn up any gunners. Bolan returned to the front door and saw João Peixoto and the two government agents near the front of the house.

Peixoto beckoned. "We did it, my friend! Not a single one got away!"

Bolan waited until he joined them to relay his news. "I might have bagged the Vulture."

"Where?"

The moment the warrior pointed, Peixoto sprinted to the corpse. Bolan trailed him, not surprised to see a look of astonishment come over the Brazilian as the body was flipped over.

"This can't be!"

"Do you know him?"

Peixoto nodded.

"It's not the Vulture." Bolan made the words a statement.

"His name is Gonzalo Hernandez. He's an arms dealer."

"He works for the Vulture?"

"No." Peixoto touched the corpse as if assuring himself it were real. "Allow me to explain." He paused. "As you know, the Vulture is the top weapons merchant in all of Brazil, perhaps in all of the Western Hemisphere. But there are many others in the trade, men equally savage, equally brutal, who would like to dethrone the Vulture and become number one themselves."

"Hernandez was one of them?"

"Yes. He was a fast riser with important connections who might have proved a match for the Vulture one day."

"So he was the Vulture's main competition," Bolan said.

"Exactly."

"And you've conveniently put him out of operation."

Peixoto glanced up. "What are you saying?"

"I suspected there was something wrong about this setup. Now I know it."

"Enlighten me, if you please."

Bolan turned so he could watch the grounds. Even though the villa seemed secure, no one had yet done a thorough search. "Didn't it strike you as strange that Roberto Garza brought you here?"

"My men tailed him."

"Only because he let them. Every other time he's lost them with ease."

The full implication made the Brazilian's mouth go slack. "You're saying Garza deliberately let us follow him? That he knew we would storm the villa and do the Vulture's dirty work for him?"

"Give credit where credit is due. Garza doesn't have the brains to cook up a scheme like this. The one behind it is the man who pulls Garza's strings."

"Mother of God! The Vulture played us like pawns." Peixoto cocked his head. "But I see a flaw in your theory. Garza had no way of knowing we would hold back until he left. He risked being caught in the cross fire."

"He couldn't very well disobey the Vulture, could he?" Bolan responded. "The way I see it, the Vulture had Garza arrange a meet with Hernandez, maybe on the pretext of including him in a lucrative arms deal. Hernandez didn't trust the Vulture, so he had Garza come to the one place Hernandez felt safe."

"His own stronghold." Peixoto shook his head in disbelief. "The Vulture is more devious than I would have believed it possible for any man to be."

"There's more."

"What do you mean?"

"That attack by the street gang. Maybe it wasn't a case of my being in the wrong place at the wrong time."

"The Vulture put them up to it? But why? Does he suspect you are not who you claimed to be?"

"Maybe." Bolan shrugged. "I only know if things had gone his way, he would have killed two birds with one stone."

"Do you understand now why we have not been able to put him out of business? How do you fight a man who is always a jump ahead of you?"

"By getting the jump on him."

"That, my friend, is easier said than done."

THE MOP-UP LASTED the remainder of the night. By the time the assistance Peixoto called for arrived, it was three in the morning. By then the villa had been thoroughly searched, and the only person found alive proved to be Hernandez's mother, the elderly woman Bolan had seen.

The sun had been up for an hour when Peixoto pulled his car to the curb in front of the Hotel Elegancia. "What will you do next?" he asked.

"Catch a few winks, then go to the room at Phillipe's."

"Are you crazy? If your cover has been blown, they will kill you on the spot."

"We don't know for sure my cover has been blown, and until we do, I'll stick to our original plan." Bolan held up a hand when the Brazilian began to protest.

"Unless you have a better idea on how we can get close to the Vulture."

The argument silenced the man. "I thought so," Bolan said, opening his door. "Don't worry. I'm not going into this with my eyes closed."

"You seek to outfox the Vulture at his own game. That is very dangerous."

"Tell me something I don't know."

Once in his room, Bolan hung out the Do Not Disturb sign, locked the door, stashed the duffel in a closet and dropped onto the bed fully clothed. Moments later he was asleep.

EVENING FOUND the warrior up, shaved, dressed and on his way to Phillipe's. Since he had every reason to expect an unfriendly reception, he packed extra hardware. In addition to the Para-Ordnance holstered under his left arm, the Tanarmi 9 mm now nestled under his right arm. And in addition to the Viper combat knife sheathed on his right ankle, he had a Gerber on his left.

Bolan didn't like walking into the lion's den again, as it were, but at least he'd be able to give the lions a run for their money if they bared their fangs. He figured he would have to wait awhile before Garza contacted him, so he was surprised to see the black Mercedes parked in front of the house and Garza standing near the door. Three hardmen and Phillipe were with the lieutenant.

Adopting a stony expression, Bolan paid off the taxi driver as Garza approached. The warrior unbuttoned his jacket and turned.

"Where have you been?" Garza demanded.

"None of your business," Bolan replied, deciding not to give an inch. He hooked his right thumb under his belt so he could draw either pistol on an instant, and met Garza's glare with one of his own. The hardmen fanned out but came no closer.

"It is too my affair," Garza responded. "When you work for our organization you are accountable for every minute of your time."

"Just my point," Bolan said calmly. "Far as I know, I haven't been hired yet."

Some of the bluster left Garza's florid face. "You would have known had you been here to receive my message as you were supposed to be."

"What message?"

"My employer has agreed to a probationary period. He will let you work with us for a while, give you a chance to prove yourself, and if you do, you are in."

"I don't much like the idea."

"Your feelings hardly matter. This is the only way you will be admitted." Garza smiled broadly, but it was devoid of warmth. "I don't see what the problem is. You came to us, not we to you. And as far as the probationary period goes, other men have been put to a similar test. It is how my employer ensures that he hires only the best."

"Can't fault him there," Bolan replied. "All right. I'll go along."

"Excellent." Garza gestured at the Mercedes. "Now if you would be so kind, we have a job to do."

"Right this minute?" Bolan asked, his brains shrieking a warning.

"Why do you think I am here? Merely to give you a hard time?" Garza laughed. "Come. You can sit in the back with me." Striding to the car, he pulled open the back door. "After you."

To refuse would ruin everything, and Bolan still hoped that his cover hadn't been blown and he might yet learn the Vulture's identity. The short hairs at his nape prickling, he slid in. As he sat back he folded his arms across his chest, contriving to slide both hands under the flaps of his jacket so he could grip the pistols.

Garza hopped in beside him and slammed the door, while the three hardmen climbed in the front. A hulking Neanderthal started the Mercedes, and they drove off.

"Now then," Garza began, "tonight you will demonstrate your loyalty by doing my employer a little favor."

"What kind of favor?"

"There is a certain person who has caused us some grief. We would be grateful if you would dispose of him for us."

"You can't do it yourselves?"

"We could. But the top man wants it done this way. Would you have me tell him that you've refused?"

"No," Bolan said. "Who is this guy I'm supposed to waste?"

"All in due time."

The warrior didn't press the issue. He didn't know what Garza was up to, but he was certain it didn't bode well for him. He would just have to stay on his toes every second.

Earlier, during the ride to Phillipe's, Bolan had noticed a growing number of people flocking into the streets, most wearing colorful costumes. Now there were even more, which was to be expected since this was a carnival night, a night of wild, rowdy celebration that put the New Orleans Mardi Gras to shame.

The streets were so choked with pedestrian traffic that the driver had a hard time of it. He seldom could go more than ten miles an hour and constantly had to lean on the horn to get laughing revelers to move aside.

Garza grew increasingly impatient. He checked his watch often and muttered curses at the celebrants.

None of the hardmen so much as glanced at Bolan. That in itself told him something. The way they kept their heads locked forward and made a show of keeping their hands in sight, either on the dash or over the back of the seat, demonstrated they were putting on a show for his benefit. They wanted him to think they were perfectly harmless.

Bolan wasn't fooled for a minute. He was leaning back, seemingly relaxed, but inwardly he was coiled to explode into action at the first hint of a threat.

Half an hour elapsed and the Mercedes traveled a mere mile. Garza leaned forward, smacked the driver on the shoulder and barked in Portuguese, "Stupid! Why do you stick to the main streets when they are so crowded? Try the side streets."

The driver obeyed, but the going was no better. If anything, the throngs were thicker, and the Mercedes crawled along.

"I should have anticipated this," Garza said to Bolan. "We will be late."

"I take it your boss won't like it if you're not on time."

"He is a stickler for punctuality, and only a fool gets him mad."

Bolan nodded at the window. "He must know what Rio is like at carnival time. Won't he let you off the hook this once?"

"You don't know him like I do. He doesn't live in Rio so—" Garza stiffened, realizing the blunder he had made. He looked sharply at Bolan. "Let's just say he is not one to accept excuses, and let it go at that."

Finally Bolan had a clue, a meager one, but a clue nonetheless. The Vulture wasn't in Rio de Janeiro. Where, then? Was he even in Brazil, or some other country?

The car turned a corner and was surrounded by gaily dressed merrymakers, some playing musical instruments, others singing lustily. A bare-breasted woman wearing what appeared to be the bottom part of a string bikini pressed her ample chest against the driver's window and called for him to stop and join the fun.

Garza punched the front seat and growled, "Enough of this nonsense! We would make better time on foot. Socorro, pull into that alley up ahead and park."

Bolan tensed. Was this a trick? Were they going to take him down once he stepped from the vehicle? He slid closer to his door and braced himself.

In a few seconds Socorro did as instructed, jamming on the brakes so hard everyone lurched forward. Garza gave him the sort of look that withered plants at ten feet, then shoved on his door and climbed out. "Hurry it up!"

The warrior got out on his side. He brought up the rear as Garza headed down the alley to the next street and bore to the left. Neither the lieutenant nor the gunners even looked his way. Garza, intent on making up for lost time, broke into a slow jog.

Crowds packed the thoroughfare. Bolan had never seen so many people in one place at one time having so much fun. Some wore outlandish garb, others went around next to naked. Some could barely stand, they were so drunk, yet the night was still young. Traffic had come to a standstill.

Moments later Garza made another turn. By taking a winding course he soon neared the harbor, away from the revelers. He entered the warehouse section that bordered the wharves, where the streets were much quieter.

When no one was looking, Bolan slipped the Para-Ordnance from its holster and tucked the pistol under his waistband on his right hip. It would permit a faster draw when the time came.

Soon the narrow streets were completely deserted. The entire population of Rio was swept up in the frenzy of the holiday. No one wanted to be among smelly warehouses in one of the dingiest sections of the city.

A huge warehouse appeared directly ahead. Garza pulled a key from his pocket and walked to a small door set in one corner. He glanced around before unlocking the door, then stood back so the others could enter first.

The warrior had a hand on the Para-Ordnance as he went in. One of the hardmen flipped a wall switch, and banks of fluorescent lights blazed to life from one end of the ceiling to the other.

Bolan blinked in the sudden glare. The warehouse reminded him of the bunkers at Hernandez's villa, only on a greater scale. Rows upon rows of stacked crates and boxes were neatly arranged, clearly labeled, containing everything from Stingers to suppressors. Where there had been enough at the villa to arm a small army, this one warehouse held enough to arm half the countries in South America.

There was another difference. The Hernandez operation had been second-rate, from the amateur gunners to the sloppily organized bunkers. Here everything was all spit and polish, a first-class act reflective of the man who ran things.

"What do you think?" Garza asked.

"I'm impressed," Bolan admitted.

"As was I, the first time I was brought here. Yet this is nothing. The tip of the iceberg only."

"Your boss has more stashed away somewhere?"

"He has many storage facilities," Garza boasted. "This one is the final export center for shipments out of the country." He chuckled. "There isn't a third-world country that hasn't received a shipment of our farm products. In fact—" Garza bobbed a chin at the crates "—in another week most everything you see will be on its way to Libya."

"And from there to terrorist groups all over the world," Bolan said.

"Precisely. The beauty of our operation is that not so much as a single bullet will be traceable to us. Believe me when I say that the man I work for is a genius in that regard."

"So what are we doing here?" Bolan asked. "I thought you wanted me to snuff someone."

"In due time," Garza replied. "Feel free to look around while I make some phone calls." He disappeared into a nearby office.

Bolan became aware that Socorro and another gunner were leaning against the wall near the door. The third man was seated on a crate close at hand. They had him boxed in unless there was another way out.

In search of one, the warrior strolled down aisle after aisle. He discovered a clear area, ten-foot square, at the very center of the warehouse. He also found another door, which was locked. Several barred, tinted windows adorned each wall, so high off the floor that no one could reach them without a ladder.

The big man was returning to the front when he thought he heard a faint scratching noise, and halted. It came from somewhere overhead. Bolan scanned the high stacks of crates but didn't see anything.

"Ah, there you are!" Garza exclaimed when the warrior returned to the hardmen. "Been admiring the goods, have you?"

"There must be fifty million dollars' worth of ordnance."

"More like twice that." Garza consulted his watch again. "Our guest of honor is due to arrive at any moment. Then we can put you to the test."

As if on cue, voices sounded outside. Socorro opened the door to admit four newcomers, one of whom was bound at the wrists and had a dirty sack covering his head.

"At last!" Garza said.

"Don't blame us," replied a thin man bearing a scar on his cheek. "The damn carnival held us up."

"As it did us. Shall we proceed?"

"Is this him?" Scarface asked, staring at Bolan.

"Yes. This is Yusuf Atasi."

"Heard a lot about you," Scarface said.

The hooded man suddenly grunted and made other sounds that showed he was gagged. He tried to pull loose from the men who held his arm and was roughly jerked erect for his effort.

"Our guest seems to be in a hurry to get this over with," Garza joked. "You would think he had more sense than that." Grasping the man's elbow, Garza steered him toward the middle of the warehouse.

Flanked by hardmen, Bolan followed. He glanced back and saw that one gunner had stayed behind to guard the door.

"Stop struggling," Garza commanded the captive, giving the man a shove that sent him sprawling. "You will live a little longer if you cooperate."

The man tried to speak but uttered muffled gibberish.

"To think you were once considered one of the best," Garza derided him. Seizing the captive by the shoulders, he hauled the man erect and gave him a hard push.

The aisle broadened at the open area. Garza slammed the captive to his knees, then gripped the top of the sack and looked at Bolan as the hardmen spread out on either side. "You wanted to know who you were to kill?" Garza yanked the hood off and smirked. "Allow me to introduce Yusuf Atasi. The *real* Yusuf Atasi."

7

To say that Mack Bolan was surprised would be an understatement. He tensed, prepared to make a last-ditch stand, when the metallic rasping of a bolt being pulled back caused him to focus on its source.

Two gunners, one armed with a Skorpion and the other a Sten MK II, had popped up on top of a stack of crates. The rest of the hardmen were unlimbering pistols and taking aim.

"Do not do anything rash," Garza advised. "You will be cut to ribbons if you so much as move a finger." He tossed the sack down and placed his hands on his hips. "Hand over your weapons and no harm will come to you. Not yet, anyway. My boss wants to have a talk with you first."

Bolan wasn't about to give up his hardware. He wouldn't go meekly to the slaughter, not while there was an ounce of strength left in him. Making a show of complying, he opened his jacket slowly, revealing the Para-Ordnance. In doing so, he pulled the jacket flap clear around behind him so he could grip the Targa. No one was to his rear, so no one saw.

"Allow me," Garza said smugly, stepping forward. "It's best not to put temptation in your hands." He snatched the .45 and hefted it. "P-14 model, I believe. What else do you have?"

"Just this," Bolan said, slowly lowering his jacket flap while holding out his other arm. The reaction was predictable. All eyes swung to his outstretched empty hand, and in that moment when they were all distracted and Garza unwittingly served as a living shield, Bolan jammed the Targa into the lieutenant's groin.

Garza blanched and glanced down. The gunners, sensing something was wrong, shifted for a better firing position but halted in midstride when their boss shrieked in Portuguese, "No! No! Stay where you are!"

"Don't do anything rash," Bolan baited the lieutenant in the same tone Garza had used on him. "Not unless you plan on giving up the ladies for life."

Beads of sweat formed on Garza's forehead, and he nervously licked his lips. "Shoot me and you will never live to reach the door."

"The way I figure it, I've got nothing to lose," Bolan said, jabbing the Targa in deeper for emphasis. "If I'm going down, you're going with me." He was watching the others, alert for any telltale flicker of motion. Would they obey Garza, or would they go for the glory? He had to seize the moment before they had time to think, to question. "Tell your men to back off and lower their guns."

Garza gulped. Fear he was unable to hide showed in his wide eyes. He hesitated, though, and looked at the Para-Ordnance, which dangled from his forefinger.

The warrior could practically read the man's mind. "Start something and you'll be caught in the cross fire."

"I can't let you leave," Garza said softly. "If I do, Carlos will kill me."

"If you don't, I'll put two shots into you before your boys take me down. That's a promise."

Only a man who possessed supreme courage would sacrifice himself for a higher cause. Garza wasn't all that brave, and the Vulture hardly qualified as a higher cause. When faced with the choice of breathing or being turned into a sieve, he picked living. "Back off, all of you! Do nothing unless I say to!"

Most of the gunners obeyed. Scarface and two others, who were in the aisle, didn't.

"You heard me!" Garza roared at them.

"And how do we explain this to the boss?" Scarface asked. "He's liable to have our heads on a platter."

"I'll take full responsibility!" Garza glanced at the gunner holding the Sten. "José, if they don't move in ten seconds, kill them."

José swung the Sten.

Tension crackled in the air. Scarface, livid, slowly lowered his pistol to his side and motioned for the other two to do the same. "Carlos will hear of this," he snapped.

That was the second time Bolan had heard that name. It could belong only to one person. But was it the Vulture's first name or his last?

"I'll tell him myself," Garza countered. He faced the warrior. "Now what, as if I can't guess?"

"Have them move out of the way. If anyone tries to be a hero, I shoot."

"You heard the bastard!"

The hardmen complied to a man, though slowly.

"Now hand over the .45," Bolan ordered.

Garza gingerly offered the pistol and the warrior took it, thumbed back the hammer and touched the barrel to the Brazilian's cheek.

"Start backing toward the front door," the warrior directed. "Easy does it." As Garza did as he was told, Bolan stayed with him.

Over the years the Executioner had been in more than his share of tight spots, and this was one of the worst. He didn't know from moment to moment if a hardman might opt to buck Garza and cut loose. Their flinty expressions were proof they wanted to.

Scarface, in particular, had the air of a man stretched to his breaking point. He fingered his pistol, his lips mashed tight, his left leg jiggling nervously.

Once past the hired killers, Bolan swung around so he could watch them. He remembered to stop when still a dozen yards from the entrance and said, "Call the guard you left there. Have him join the rest."

"You'll never get away with this."

"I've heard it all before. Just do as I told you." Bolan tapped the .45 on the tip of Garza's nose.

"Orlando, come here! Hands in the air! Pronto!"

The man was as obedient as the rest. He came, arms elevated, and glared at the warrior as he walked by.

Swiftly Bolan backpedaled to the door, dragging the lieutenant after him. Pausing, he shoved the .22 into his pocket. He could see Scarface and a few of the others standing where he had left them. So far they had behaved themselves, but that was about to change. He tested the knob, then threw the door open.

"We will nail you, *senhor*," Garza rasped. "No matter where you go, how deep a hole you dig, we will hunt you down and exterminate you."

"You'll try." Bolan took a step outside, the Para-Ordnance leveled.

"Run, you bastard!" Garza ranted. "Our men will be on you before you go two blocks. They will fill you with lead and feed your body to the sharks, but I will spit on it first.'' Then the Brazilian made his move, launching himself at his adversary.

Bolan saw it coming and sidestepped. He triggered two rounds, then took off in a flat-out run, veering to the right to hug the buildings rather than be exposed to hostile guns in the middle of the deserted street. He reached the end of the block as a black car bearing the gunners rounded the corner. The man with the Sten opened up, lead splattering against the wall and missing Bolan by inches.

The warrior pumped his legs. He had to find a phone and tell Peixoto about the warehouse. A swift raid might net crucial intel about the Vulture. But this was the warehouse district, and pay phones were few and far between.

In the distance he could hear noisy revelers. Thanks to the carnival, Bolan had one less problem to worry about. There were no pedestrians left in the immediate area, no innocents to be hurt if the gunners caught up with him before he could lose himself in the crowds.

The black car screamed around the block, the engine growling as the driver pressed the pedal to the floor.

As Bolan passed an office building, he tossed a quick glance over a shoulder to see the hardman with the Skorpion poke out the front window. The warrior dived, smacking the pavement hard as the weapon cut loose with a sustained burst that splintered wood and shattered glass. Then the car swept by and the Executioner stood up.

He spotted an alley a few yards distant. A quick jog took him beneath a fire escape. He leaped up and grabbed the bottom rung. With a heave the warrior brought his feet up, then crouched and drew the .45 and the 9 mm pistols.

Moments later the sedan filled the alley. The driver and the man with the Skorpion were looking right and left for a sign of their quarry when they should have been looking up.

The Executioner brought both the Para-Ordnance and the Tanarmi into play, blasting six shots in half as many seconds.

The windshield dissolved in a spray of glass. Clutching his face, the driver collapsed and the sedan slewed into the left-hand wall. It careened off, then plowed into the opposite wall below the fire escape.

As soon as the car smashed to a stop, Bolan jumped, landing flat-footed on the roof. The passenger door opened and out sprang Skorpion. Wobbly, shaken by the crash, the man tried to bring the weapon into target acquisition. The .45 boomed once, and the gunner dropped to the ground, permanently out of the play.

Shouts rose in the street, and more killers entered the alley.

Bolan vaulted from the roof to the hood a heartbeat before a lethal hailstorm peppered the wall. His feet touched ground and he sprinted down the alley, knowing he had to get out before more gunners blocked the other end.

But there were no hardmen on the far side. Once in the open, Bolan swung left. His pursuers would count on him making for the center of Rio and would spread out accordingly, but he had a better idea. At the next intersection he turned toward Guanabara Bay. He was barely out of sight before the gunners gained the street, as testified to by their yells. They couldn't understand where he had gotten to so quickly.

The warrior ducked into a shadowed doorway and listened to the slap of feet as the bloodthirsty pack took the bait. When the sounds had faded, he stepped out and headed for the wharves.

The warrior jogged in the direction of the swimming beaches. There would be plenty of people, and he'd be able to blend among them. With luck he should be able to find a telephone.

A damp breeze blew off the bay. In the distance a ship approached, its lights like oversize fireflies in the darkness.

Bolan replaced the pistols in their holsters in case he should stumble on a civilian. The last thing he needed was to have the police detain him. There would be countless questions, and it might be hours before Peixoto could bail him out.

Suddenly a figure materialized directly ahead. Bolan instinctively reached for the .45, then just as swiftly lowered his arm when he recognized the uniform of a Rio cop. He slowed to a casual walk, but it was too late. He'd caught the cop's attention and the man was angling to intercept him.

"Senhor! Um momento, faca favor."

Bolan summoned a carefree smile and lifted a hand in friendly greeting, playing the part of a typical tourist. "Hello, Officer. I'm American. Do you happen to speak English?"

The cop was middle-aged, experienced. He studied the big man, then said, "I do. Who are you, *senhor,* and what are you doing out here all by yourself?"

"Tony Bianco, at your service," Bolan said, putting enough of a lilt into his voice and movements to give the impression he had downed one drink too many.

"You have strayed from the carnival, yes?"

"Needed to clear the old noggin, if you get my drift. Thought a quiet walk would do the trick."

"You must be careful, Senhor Bianco. Some parts of the city are not all that safe at this time of night."

"I'll remember that."

The policeman gazed past Bolan. "Have you heard any unusual noises in the past few minutes?"

"Noises?"

"Gunshots, perhaps?"

"I should hope not. I came to Rio to party, not to be mugged."

The cop scratched his chin in thought. "A watchman called in and reported hearing some shots. If you ask me, all he heard were firecrackers." He shrugged. "Well, I will be on my way if you would be so kind as to show me your identification papers first."

Bolan presented the phony ID and passport provided by Brognola.

"All appears to be in order." The cop pointed at the bright glow that framed downtown Rio like a halo. "You should go back now and enjoy yourself."

"Thank you. I will." Bolan pocketed his papers, and the policeman moved around him to continue on. Suddenly there was a loud splat, as of a fist striking soft flesh, and something heavy rammed into the Executioner's back, nearly bowling him over. He crouched and whirled and saw the cop lying dead, a bullet hole in the temple.

The warrior hadn't heard a shot. Whoever fired was using a suppressor and would be hard to locate. He kissed the sand, heard a buzz overhead. Springing up, he slanted toward a cluster of trees bordering the beach.

Another round kicked up sand close by. He zigzagged, never going in a straight line for more than a step or two. If there were more shots, he didn't hear anything. Then he was at the trees, behind a curved trunk.

A slug tore into the bole so close it sent slivers into Bolan's chin when he peered out. Crouch-walking, he made his way through the grove to a sidewalk.

Ascertaining that he was in the clear, Bolan rose and ran. He hadn't gone more than a block when he spotted a public phone across the street. Slipping a hand into his pocket for change, he raced across the road and was passing between two parked cars when a wiry shape tackled him, steely arms banding around his legs.

The warrior went down. His assailant clawed onto his back and got an arm around his neck. Bolan tried to flip the man off, but it was no go. He could feel incredible pressure being applied to his windpipe, knew he'd be dead soon if he didn't do something.

Bolan reared up, then dropped backward, driving the hardman against a car. At the same time he speared both elbows around and in. There was a crack, a grunt and the grip on his neck loosened.

The warrior tucked forward, heaving his attacker face-first to the ground. The man grabbed for a pistol at his waist, but Bolan was faster. Two slugs from the Tanarmi cored the gunner's head, knocking him backward, spurting brains.

Bolan darted to the phone. As his hand swooped for the receiver, the handset blew apart. Twisting, he finally glimpsed the sniper, a hardcase with a rifle, maybe a Ruger by the looks of it. The man was taking a bead.

Only the cars offered immediate cover, and Bolan didn't hesitate, beating the next shot by the blink of an eye. He couldn't afford to stay there, to let the sniper pin him down long enough for the rest to close in.

Breaking into the open, Bolan banged half the clip at the sniper, who ducked behind a building. He raced around the next corner, then stopped abruptly. Squatting, he waited to see if the sniper would do the same or would approach the corner quietly and slowly.

Evidently the man was overeager. Bolan heard the patter of footsteps and had the 9 mm pistol ready when the sniper showed. Two shots to the head was all it took.

At that moment several couples in costume happened on the scene. One of the women screamed, and one of the men bellowed for the police.

Bolan got out of there in a hurry, the Tanarmi going under his waistband. Within a block he encountered more revelers. Within three blocks there were dozens. He stopped running and walked, threading among the happy throngs. Before long he was hemmed in on all sides, the best camouflage a man could ask for.

By Bolan's reckoning there were four gunners left—Scarface, Sten, Socorro and one other. He couldn't see them dogging him all the way into the heart of the city, but he couldn't take it for granted that they wouldn't, either. So when he happened on a vendor selling masks, he bought one in the likeness of a jaguar.

Five minutes elapsed. Ten. Bolan had not seen any sign of his enemies. Nor had he found a working telephone yet.

Since the warrior had been trained as a soldier to always take the high ground, whether while reconnoitering or in a firefight, when he saw a street lamp he climbed it for a better view. The carnival-goers were too wrapped up in antics of their own to notice.

Trying to pick one person out of that swirling mass of riotous humanity was nearly impossible. Bolan saw no one who aroused his suspicion. Sliding down, he merged into the flow.

Twice the warrior found telephones and both times they were being used. He waited at the second one, but the woman was in no hurry.

Ultimately Bolan determined to hoof it all the way to the Hotel Elegancia. A quick call and Peixoto and the tactical squad would pick him up on their way to the warehouse.

Getting there took much longer than Bolan had anticipated. The streets surrounding the hotel were a virtual madhouse. Often he had to force his way through packed crowds or pry himself from the arms of a woman wanting to dance or kiss.

The hotel lobby was empty save for the desk clerk, who wore the hangdog look of a man missing out on all the fun. He merely nodded as Bolan paused at the desk long enough to drop the mask in a trash can, then stared longingly at the festivities.

The warrior walked by a massive, ornate marble column and stabbed the button for his floor. The clang of the elevator as it started down to retrieve him, combined with the din outside, was enough to drown out any other sounds. Consequently he didn't realize someone had been lurking on the far side of the column until the elevator doors parted and he began to enter. It was then, out of the corner of an eye, he registered a hawkish shadow streaking toward him.

The warrior's hand closed on the butt of the 9 mm pistol at the same moment cool metal touched his nape and a heavily accented voice spoke in his ear.

"Do that and die, pig! There is nothing I would like more than to kill you, but Carlos wants you for himself."

It was Scarface. The killer shoved Bolan against the back wall and briskly stripped him of the Tanarmi, the Para-Ordnance and the Targi. "You are a walking armory," Scarface grumbled as the doors closed and the car rose.

Bolan held his peace. He still had the knives, but they were useless unless he could get his hands on one, which the hardman wasn't about to let him do. Scarface was more professional than the rest, a skilled cutthroat who wouldn't relax his guard for an instant.

"Are you surprised? You didn't know we had found your lair, did you?"

Bolan was grabbed, roughly swung around and shoved against the doors.

"Garza was a fool to take you so lightly! I would not have, not after what you did to the Eagles."

"The gang Carlos sent to kill me?"

"You are smarter than you look. Only it was not him. It was our boss."

The car climbed slowly. It was now halfway between the second and third floors. Bolan stood with his arms outstretched, his palms against the doors. He could see the control panel near his left hand and the red button that meant the difference to him between life and death. And when Scarface glanced up at the floor indicator arrow above the doors, he punched that button.

To Scarface's credit, he tried to get off a shot but the jolt of the car lurching to a halt threw him off balance and he fell back against the rear wall.

The warrior turned and pounced, his right knee up. It caught Scarface in the chest, dazing him. Bolan slashed a hand at his adversary's wrist, and the blow sent the killer's gun flying. Scarface retaliated with a punch to the throat that Bolan blocked. When the Brazilian followed up with a roundhouse, Bolan ducked under the fist and planted one of his own in the hardman's gut.

Scarface was nothing if not tough. He absorbed the punch without flinching, shifted and suddenly had the Para-Ordnance in his hand. His scar flushed red with anger, he lunged, pressed the muzzle of the .45 to the warrior's chest and sneered as he squeezed the trigger.

8

The Executioner had learned his lethal craft in the killing fields of Vietnam. He was an expert marksman, the best of the best. He could draw a pistol, release the safety and fire in a fraction of the time it took most men. Because he was so skilled, he used the safeties on his pistols as a matter of course.

Not all men did. The average Mob or free-lance gunner seldom did. By leaving the safeties on their weapons off, they could get off a shot that much sooner.

Of course, there were drawbacks to the practice. If jarred hard enough, a pistol might go off. If dropped, a man could be injured. But that didn't stop the gunners from doing it.

Scarface belonged to that school. He seldom used a safety himself, and he made the mistake of assuming no one else did, either. When he pulled the .45, he didn't bother to check the safety, didn't even touch it. The look on his face when he squeezed the trigger and nothing happened was almost comical.

But Mack Bolan wasn't laughing. His hand compacted into a tight wedge, he employed a karate blow to the sternum. Scarface staggered, and in order not to give the killer a chance to recover, the warrior chopped him across the throat.

Stunned but still game, Scarface reeled and tried to find the safety on the .45 through a haze of blood and pain.

The Executioner brought up his right leg, not to kick, but to grasp the Viper. The blade sliced smoothly into Scarface's ribs, two times in succession. After the second stab the hardman arched his spine, gasped and collapsed to the floor of the elevator.

Bolan caught the Para-Ordnance, then reclaimed all his guns and added Scarface's to his collection. He removed the man's jacket so he could mop up the blood.

After stuffing the jacket under the dead man's shirt, Bolan hit the button to bring the car to his floor. Quickly he threw Scarface over his shoulder, hiding the crimson chest stain. Should anyone see them and ask, he would explain that Scarface was stone drunk.

The elevator hissed open onto an empty corridor. Bolan had to fiddle with his lock to get the door open. Once inside, he flicked on the lights and headed for the bathroom. The disturbing sight on the living room carpet stopped him in his tracks.

João Peixoto lay sprawled in violent death. His hands were clenched, as if to strike. Five bullet holes were evenly spaced over his heart.

Drops of blood told Bolan the story. Peixoto had been seated in a chair, waiting for his return. The door had either been unlocked then or Scarface picked the lock and slipped inside. The first bullet had hit Peixoto as he stood. The shot had to have been fatal, but somehow he had taken a couple more steps and been shot four more times before collapsing.

Bolan stared at the body awhile, then dragged both corpses into the bathroom and placed them one on top of the other in the tub. "Sorry, friend," he said softly as he pulled the shower curtain closed.

A trip to the closet revealed the duffel hadn't been rifled. Bolan added Scarface's piece to the arsenal, slung the bag over his shoulder and walked to the door.

The time had come for the Executioner to take off the kid gloves. He had tried Brognola's plan to infiltrate the Vulture's organization and it had backfired. He had cooperated with the Brazilian authorities, and the results had been disastrous. Now a good man had died in his stead.

Mack Bolan was going to do things his way from then on. No more playing patsy with the hardmen. No more letting his judgment be swayed by well-meaning government agents. He was going to take the Vulture down, and take him down hard.

The clerk cocked an eyebrow when Bolan retrieved the jaguar mask, but made no comments. In the street the carnival still raged. The drinking, the singing, the sex would go on all night. By morning there wouldn't be one person in a thousand who didn't have a hangover.

Donning the mask, the warrior once again mingled with the multitudes. He knew there'd be backup, so he steered close to a building and stopped to check for tails. Scarface wouldn't have gone to the hotel alone. There had to be another gunner or two. Look as he might, however, the big man failed to find one. Everyone he saw was in costume. He hurried on, the only grim soul in the madcap city, it seemed.

Every so often Bolan would look back. In the jumble of crazy costumes it was hard to keep track of any single one, but he did notice a huge gorilla that was always there, half a block away, never more, never less. The first time he saw the giant ape, he didn't think much of it. The second time, he grew suspicious. The third time he fingered the .45.

Bolan picked up the pace, searching for an empty street he could lure the gorilla into. He might as well have been searching for a needle in a haystack.

At an intersection the warrior turned right. Steps flanking a building led to basement level, and he quickly dashed to a niche below and hid in the shadows. By craning his neck he could keep an eye on the sidewalk. Moments later the gorilla strode past, looking both ways.

Bolan stayed put for a while before walking to street level. The gorilla had disappeared. He changed the duffel from his left shoulder to his right and continued toward the warehouse district.

Eventually the crowds thinned. The warrior saw a taxi but didn't hail it. For what he had planned, total secrecy was called for.

Police lights were flashing near the beach, where the cop had been shot. From two blocks away Bolan observed officers with flashlights scouring the area for clues. Little did they know they were wasting their time. Bolan doubted they would find anything other than a shell casing, if that. There would be no leads to direct their investigation to the Vulture's ring. It was up to him to avenge that cop, and avenge him he would.

In short order Bolan spotted the warehouse. He swung to the south of the structure and once on the wharves made his way to a pile of busted crates near the rear. The tinted windows prevented him from seeing if lights were on inside.

Unzipping the duffel, Bolan loaded for bear. He also pulled out two Thunder strips, detonation cord and a small detonator. The mask went into the bag.

The doors fronting the wharf were corrugated, and too massive to bother with. Bolan jogged down an alley to the street. A peek disclosed a black limo parked at the curb, guarded by a hulk of a man. A moment later the door opened, and out walked a half-dozen hardmen, and two others. One was Yusuf Atasi, still bound but no longer gagged, his face a study in stark fear. The other was a tall, rugged man in his forties, someone Bolan hadn't seen before. Dressed in an expensive suit and polished boots, he had an air of authority about him.

The man in the suit spoke in English to Atasi.

"I would let you ride up front with me, but in your state I'm afraid you might soil your pants and ruin the upholstery."

"Please," the terrorist said, "what have I done to deserve this treatment? I came here willingly, of my own accord."

"Your second mistake."

Anger made Atasi brave. "My only mistake, Rivas, was in thinking your employer is a man of honor."

"I will be sure to tell Carlos that," Rivas retorted, nodding at the hulk, who promptly walked to the trunk of the limo. "It amazes me that you are taking this so personal."

Atasi swallowed hard as the trunk was opened. "How else should I take this betrayal?"

"You are a fine one to talk after the damage you have caused our organization."

"I have done nothing!"

"Garza would disagree, were he still alive," Rivas said. "We have lost quite a few good men because of you."

"I didn't kill them."

"True, you didn't pull the trigger. But someone is on to us, and Carlos believes you are to blame."

Atasi tried to resist as two hardmen grasped his arms and forced him toward the trunk. "I'm not! I swear by all that is holy!"

"An anarchist like you? For shame," Rivas taunted, and laughed heartily.

Atasi was roughly shoved into the trunk. He tried to rise and received a ringing slap across the face. Then the gag was reapplied.

Chuckling, Rivas walked over and placed a hand on the trunk lid. "Make yourself comfortable. The ride will not take long, and by tomorrow morning we will be at Taguarí."

He slammed the lid. The hulk hastened to hold open a back door for him. Rivas was about to slide in when he paused and addressed two hardmen standing near the warehouse in rapid-fire Portuguese.

Bolan caught the gist of it. Since the warehouse had been compromised, the munitions were being relocated. Trucks would be there by midmorning. If people who had no business being there showed up, they were to be killed.

The rest of the gunners piled into the limo and the car pulled out. Bolan let it go. Eliminating Rivas might cause the Vulture to head for parts unknown out of fear the authorities were closing in. It was better to let the Vulture think he had everything under control, that there was no reason to make himself scarce.

The two hardmen waited until the limo had disappeared, then they went inside. Bolan heard the lock click. He stalked from the alley and crouched in front of the door. There wasn't much of a gap at the bottom, but it was enough to let him slide two Thunder strips underneath. He quickly unwound the det cord, retreated around the corner and shouted at the top of his lungs. He set off the Thunder strip a second later.

There was a loud *whomp*. The warrior was at the shattered door before the dust settled. He kicked a panel out of the way and barged inside to find the two hardmen on the floor. Both had been going to investigate the noise and had been caught in the blast, just as Bolan had intended.

One man appeared dead, blood trickling from his nose. The other was trying to unleather a pistol, his hand shaking so badly he couldn't get a grip.

Bolan grabbed the pistol and flung it far down the aisle. Grabbing the front of the gunner's shirt, he hauled the man over by the office and propped him against the wall. *"Fala Ingles?"*

The gunner spit at him, then lunged at the warrior's weapon.

A quick rap on the man's temple with the butt of the Uzi rendered the man unconscious.

Bolan strode to the office door, but didn't bother to use the knob. A swift kick did the trick. He went straight to a desk and rummaged through the drawers, which yielded manifests, receipts and tally sheets, but not a clue as to where Taguarí might be.

Straightening, Bolan noticed a small map of Brazil on the opposite wall. He examined it closely and eventually found what he was looking for.

Taguarí was a small town situated on the Sucuriú River, far to the northwest of Rio de Janeiro. It was at the base of the Mato Grosso Plateau, perhaps one of the least explored regions on the entire planet. Small wonder no one had been able to track the Vulture to his lair. It was as far off the beaten path as a person could get.

A scraping sound drew Bolan to the office door. The gunner had revived and was sitting up. On spotting the Executioner the man stupidly went for his gun. A single shot from the Uzi snapped his head back and he slumped down again.

Bolan stepped to the office telephone and dialed the operator. When she answered, he asked for the police. In his best Portuguese he gave the officer who came on the line the address of the warehouse and added, *"Bomba! Bomba!"* to speed them along.

Hanging up, the warrior turned to go. He was only halfway through the turn when immense arms encircled him from behind and he was lifted bodily off the floor. Before he could tilt the Uzi and fire, Bolan was rammed into the wall with such force his ears rang.

"Bastardo!"

Bolan struggled in vain. It was like being in the grip of an industrial vise. He was thrown against the desk, head-first. Stars exploded before his eyes and he felt the Uzi ripped from his grasp, as was the INA. His vision cleared and he saw the gunner named Socorro looming above him, dressed in a gorilla suit. The mask was off, but Socorro's face was no improvement. Contorted in blood lust, the giant snarled as he bent and clamped both enormous hands onto Bolan's neck.

The warrior was hoisted into the air and shaken. Fingers as thick as crowbars gouged into his flesh, cutting off his breath.

Bolan raised his right leg high enough for him to draw the Viper. Socorro, grumbling like an enraged bear, batted the knife loose and suddenly spun, hurling Bolan through the doorway. The warrior landed on the concrete floor, scraping his elbows and forearms. He tried to bring the Para-Ordnance into play, but the hulking brute was on him first, bending his arm at an impossible angle. Having no other choice, he dropped the .45.

Socorro released his hold, reared back and sneered. A sadistic gleam in his eyes, he drew back a ponderous leg to kick.

Bolan was ready. He threw himself aside, spun and delivered a sweep kick of his own to the back of the giant's legs.

Socorro grunted as his feet were knocked out from under him. Landing on his back, he twisted, trying to seize the warrior.

But Bolan was already in motion. Scrabbling backward, he drew the Tanarmi. He aimed as the hardman rose, firing four times as the gunner charged, three more times before Socorro fell to the floor, dead.

Sirens howled in the distance. Bolan had to get out of there before the police arrived, but first there was something he had to do. Retrieving his weapons, he hurried down the aisle until he came to a certain pallet he remembered from his previous visit. Piled on it were small square packs bearing the stenciled designation M-72 A-1. He swung one over a shoulder and sprinted to the street, in search of a telephone.

HAL BROGNOLA HADN'T LIKED the idea of Bolan going in alone. But as the warrior had pointed out, in the time it would take Grimaldi to fly down from the States, he could be well into the interior. And contacting higher-ups in the Brazilian government was out of the question. Bolan didn't know who he could trust now that João Peixoto was dead.

So dawn found Bolan west of Rio at a small airport, a run-down affair boasting an ancient cargo plane fitted with pontoons. A small, weathered man in overalls bustled out of the ramshackle office to greet him.

"I'm Mike Belasko," Bolan introduced himself.

"The man who called about my plane, yes? I am Rui." The man pointed proudly at the aircraft. "I call her *Dolores,* after my wife. As you can see, she can land on water or land, just as I told you."

One of the struts, Bolan saw, was in bad need of repair. "Will she hold up to a long trip?"

"How long, *senhor?*"

"I want to go to Taguarí."

The pilot whistled. "You want to go to the end of the world, *senhor.* Hardly anyone ever goes there."

"Can we get to Taguarí in one piece?" Bolan persisted.

"Yes. It is over four hundred miles, so I will have to refill on the way back. That will cost you extra."

"You'll only be taking me one way."

The pilot did a double take. "You want to *stay* in Taguarí? Well, if that is what you wish. When would you like to leave?"

"Now."

The plane's gas tank had to be topped off, and Rui made a show of inspecting the engine. There was barely room enough in the cramped cabin for two people let alone Bolan's gear and the supplies the pilot brought along. As *Dolores* took wing, rattling like the antique heap she was, Bolan had a twinge of regret that he hadn't taken Brognola up on the offer to send Grimaldi down.

Rui proved to be an adept pilot, and talkative. In colorful detail he told the history of Brazil since the days of the Portuguese, and when he ran out of information he went on at length about the female conquests he had made.

Bolan tolerated the chatter because Rui had one redeeming feature—the pilot didn't pry into the warrior's business. Making himself as comfortable as he could in a seat that was as hard as a rock, the Executioner shut out the drone and gazed on the lush scenery below.

For the first hour an endless string of coffee plantations passed beneath them. Then there were scattered ranches and farms. In due course the dwellings dwindled, to be replaced by raw wilderness, tropical jungle mixed with stretches of savanna. Every so often an isolated town would appear.

"Do you know much about the jungle, *senhor?*" Rui asked at one point.

Bolan thought of Vietnam and Cambodia and nodded.

"You do? That is good. The jungle is no place for city-bred people. It eats them alive. I should know. I crashed once and barely got out with my skin."

"Try not to crash this time."

Rui laughed. "I will do my best. But you need not worry. I have a parachute on board." His chest swelled. "I packed it myself."

"Ever used it?"

"No. But my cousin, who sold it to me, assures me there are no holes."

Several hours later Rui pressed his nose to the side window and commented, "Look for a town. We should be coming up on Sanariapo. I must stop there awhile."

"To refill?"

"To check my oil. The pressure gauge does not read right, and I have a small leak."

The airstrip at Sanariapo was a dirt track bordered by dense vegetation. *Dolores* bounced three times before coming to rest near a shed. Rui turned her to be ready for takeoff and remarked, "You might as well stretch your legs, *senhor*. This will take a few minutes."

Bolan saw only one other aircraft, a sleek, modern hydroplane parked a hundred yards off. It seemed as out of place there as a Rolls-Royce would be. He strolled over and was making a circuit of the craft when a man in a panama hat, casual clothes, and carrying a cane, approached.

"Do you know much about planes, *senhor?*"

"Enough to know this one is as fine as they come. Is it yours?" Bolan asked.

"Yes. My pride and joy, you might say." The man extended a hand. "Allow me to introduce myself. Renato Cortez."

"Mike Belasko."

"I saw you through the window and came out to talk. It is rare to see an American here."

"You could tell my nationality just by looking at me?"

Cortez shrugged. "I have traveled much, *senhor*. After a while such things come naturally." He paused. "Are you staying here long?"

"No."

"What a pity. I would have enjoyed making conversation. Well, if you should change your mind, visit me in the bar." Cortez touched the brim of his hat and headed toward town.

Bolan walked over to the cargo plane. There was no sign of Rui so he walked to the shed. It was empty. Stepping outside, he called the pilot's name but received no answer. He stepped to the dirt road and scanned it from end to end. Cortez and an elderly woman were the only two people in sight.

Puzzled, Bolan went back to *Dolores*. He checked the cabin, then stood next to the propeller and surveyed the airstrip. It seemed impossible, yet there was no denying the evidence. His pilot had disappeared.

9

The Executioner had hoped to reach the interior without alerting the Vulture. A local plane, he had reasoned, would be less likely to attract unwanted attention at stops along the way. He'd planned on being flown to within a day's hike of Taguarí, then have Rui set down on the Sucuriú River. But something had gone wrong.

Bolan studied the ground around the plane. There were no scuff marks, no signs at all of a struggle. Whatever had happened to Rui had happened too swiftly for him to resist or call out.

The nearest cover was a wall of undergrowth to the rear of the shed. Bolan headed that way but stopped suddenly when he saw fresh drops of blood dotting the grass. Drawing the .45, he darted to the side of the shed. When no shots sounded, he sped into the vegetation and squatted.

Finding Rui was no problem. His brightly colored shirt stood out in sharp contrast against the green background.

Bolan's lips compressed as he stared at the dead man's vacant expression. The cause of death was obvious. The pilot had been speared through the back by a long, razor-sharp weapon, the blow delivered with precision right through his heart. It was doubtful the man knew what had hit him.

Pivoting, Bolan went to the plane and climbed in the cabin. He took the mini-Uzi out of the duffel and stuffed two magazines in his pocket. Hanging on a hook was a poncho he appropriated. Slipping it on, he hopped down and headed for Sanariapo.

The road was now deserted. The humidity and high temperature raised beads of sweat on Bolan's brow after he had hiked a few hundred feet. He held the Uzi loosely under the poncho, on the lookout for an ambush. None materialized, and on rounding a bend he saw the town.

A strong wind would have blown every building over. A single old car was parked on the dusty street. Several dogs lolled in the shade, as did several men on chairs. Animals and townsmen alike looked up as the warrior strode toward the bar, and as one they slipped away.

Bolan moved closer to the buildings on his right. Many had broken windows, one no door. He ducked into a narrow alley, sprinting its full length.

The rear door to the bar was unlocked. He opened it slowly to keep the rusty hinges from squeaking. A short hall led to an empty kitchen. Beyond, another short hall took him to the main room.

Five armed men stood at the front, three next to windows, one on either side of the door. Renato Cortez was among them, his cane in hand. No customers were present, nor a bartender.

"Where is he?" whispered a man holding a double-barreled shotgun.

"He will be here soon," Cortez assured him.

"You should have killed him at the plane."

"Not this one. There was no taking him by surprise."

Bolan glided to the end of the bar. He raised the Uzi and trained it on Shotgun just as one of the others happened to glance back and see him.

"Son of a bitch! Behind us!"

To a man, the five gunners whirled. The warrior let the Uzi introduce itself, the shots stitching Shotgun from crotch to throat. A second hardman, caught in the act of aiming a revolver, screamed as a burst of hot lead flung him through a window.

Bolan dropped below the counter, heard slugs tear into the wood and boots pound the floorboards as the gunners fled. Turning, he dashed into the hall and kept going until he was outside. He ran toward the end of town, slanting to the street when he reached the last building.

Cortez and the two hardmen were backpedaling in his direction, Cortez with a drawn pistol. They were clustered together, sitting ducks. But Bolan wanted one of them alive so he changed to semiauto, took careful aim and dropped the two hardmen with head shots.

The survivor whirled, saw the Uzi pointed at him and immediately threw down his pistol. "Don't shoot!" he cried. "It is over!"

"Not by a damn sight," Bolan growled. He wagged the Uzi. "Get your hands up and get over here."

"Whatever you want! Just don't shoot!"

Bolan nodded at Cortez's cane. "You're forgetting something."

"But I need this to walk. My foot—"

The warrior took a stride and tore the cane from Cortez's hand. He gave the handle a sharp twist and the wooden sheath fell off to reveal the glistening blade. Without missing a beat he stabbed the cane an inch into

Cortez's thigh. It wasn't deep, just enough to make Cortez yelp and stumble backward.

"Damn you!"

Bolan made as if to thrust again.

"No! No!" Cortez cried, clutching his thigh. "Why did you spare me? What do you want?"

"A replacement." Bolan heaved the cane, gripped Cortez by the wrist and gave him a shove. "Start walking."

"Where?"

"The airport."

"Why?"

"You ask too many questions," Bolan said. "Move it or lose it." As Cortez limped westward, he checked behind them. Apparently none of the town's inhabitants was of a mind to interfere.

"How did you know I was waiting for you?"

"I'm not stupid."

"He'll get you, you know. Carlos will have a fitting reception set up at Casa Cordoba."

"House of Cordoba? Is that his last name? Thanks for the information."

The sarcasm provoked an oath. "You are not as smart as you think you are, mister. Carlos knew you would come for him. He sent me to all the airports between Taguarí and Rio to ask our contacts to keep an eye out for anyone answering your description."

"And you hit the jackpot," Bolan said.

"He has been playing with you all along," Cortez boasted. "You do not stand a chance. Take my advice and go back to America while you can still breathe."

"I have business to settle with Cordoba first."

"You must have a death wish."

The airport lay deserted. Bolan had Cortez lie on his belly, then opened the door to the old cargo plane and pulled out his duffel and the pack he had taken from the warehouse. "Carry these to your plane."

Sullenly Cortez rose and picked them up. "You can't be thinking what I think you are thinking. You will get us both killed."

"Cordoba won't shoot at one of his own aircraft. You're going to take me right to his doorstep, and if you're lucky I'll let you live."

"He will suspect and have us shot out of the sky. You don't know him like I do. The man never takes anything for granted."

"That makes two of us. Get in."

The amphibian was much roomier than Rui's clunker. The seats were padded, the cabin soundproofed. Bolan placed his gear on the long back seat and strapped himself into the copilot's seat. The Uzi rested on his lap.

"I need fuel," Cortez claimed.

"Start up."

Cortez hesitated until the warrior lifted the Uzi. Reluctantly he flipped a few switches, set the throttle and turned the engine over.

Bolan leaned over to check the fuel gauge, which indicated the plane had a full tank. He placed the muzzle of the Uzi against the pilot's temple, making the man flinch. "Care to lie to me again?"

"No," Cortez snapped.

"Let's go."

The furious hardman revved the engine several times, reset the throttle, then adjusted the flaps and taxied onto the dirt runway.

Bolan never took his eyes off the man. Once they were airborne he replaced the partially spent magazine in the Uzi. While doing so he saw a folded map in a pocket on the door. On examining it he found it to be an old map of the region with all the pertinent landmarks on their route highlighted. He placed it in his own pocket.

"What do you want with that?" Cortez asked testily.

"You never know when something might come in handy."

"It is the only navigation aid I have. There are no air navigation charts for the area we are going into. It is too remote."

"Which makes it perfect for Carlos Cordoba," Bolan said in order to prompt the pilot into revealing more about the Vulture's operation.

"No one would think to look for him so far from civilization," Cortez agreed, taking the bait. "He lives like a king, in luxury most men can only dream about."

"It must be hard for him to keep his operation running smoothly with his lines of communication stretched so thin."

"For anyone other than Carlos it would be a problem, but he thinks of everything. He has his own satellite dish on his property and a relay system of shortwave and radiophone points set up from Taguarí to places all over Brazil."

"A stickler for organization, is he?"

"You do not know the half of it. Working for him is like being in the army. Which is to be expected since he was—" Cortez stopped abruptly, biting his lower lip.

"Interesting," Bolan said. "So Cordoba is ex-military. That explains a lot."

"I never said any such thing."

"You didn't have to."

The pilot glowered.

"He's an ex-officer," Bolan guessed, "and he must still have high-level military contacts, people he's bought who help hide his operation from the civilian authorities."

Cortez made no reply.

"Not that it matters. His days of selling arms are numbered."

"You seriously think you can bring him down all by yourself? One man against a small army?"

"All it takes is one shot."

"You will never get close enough."

"Just get me to Taguarí and I'll find a way."

Cortez glanced sharply at the warrior, his brow knit. For a moment a crafty spark flared in his eyes, then he assumed a sober air and commented, "Whatever you say. I never argue with anyone holding a gun on me."

Neither spoke a word after that for a long while. An unending carpet of jungle unfolded underneath them, broken here and there by isolated outposts and small towns. In due time they came on the Sucuriú River and paralleled its sluggish course.

Bolan had time to do some thinking. There was a chance that someone in Sanariapo had radioed ahead and alerted Cordoba that he was coming. He would have to put down as close to the town as he could without being detected and make a swift, hard probe to find the Vulture's base before the defenders could rally.

Suddenly Cortez hissed. He was looking straight ahead, at the horizon.

Bolan did the same and saw a small black speck. It rapidly grew in size, materializing into the shape of another plane. "A friend of yours?" he asked.

"Cordoba has five planes at his disposal. It could be any one of them. We should turn around, try to lose it."

"No. They're bound to radio you. When they do, you'd better convince them that nothing is wrong." Bolan raised the Uzi.

A minute elapsed, but the radio was silent. Bolan studied the oncoming craft, trying to identify the type by its configuration. Before he could, the plane arced high into the clouds and was lost.

"I do not like this!" Cortez said.

Bolan was feeling a little uneasy himself. He leaned forward to peer up at the sky above them but saw no trace of the other aircraft. "How much farther to Taguarí?" he inquired.

"Perhaps ten minutes, no more."

"I want you to put down on the river in five."

"If we live that long," Cortez muttered.

As if to underscore the pilot's point, there was a series of metallic shrieks and the amphibian vibrated violently. Heavy-caliber slugs ripped through the cabin roof and thudded into the floor, missing Cortez by a hair.

"Lose them!" Bolan commanded.

Cortez needed no encouragement. He banked the amphibian into a steep dive, angling for the treetops. From above and behind them more rounds punched into the cabin and the wings. The amphibian shook wildly.

Bolan twisted, seeking a glimpse of their attacker. He tried to open the door, intending to discourage the opposition with a few bursts from the Uzi, but the wind sheer slammed the door shut in his face.

The jungle raced up to meet them. Cortez was as rigid as a board. He had the engine roaring at its peak.

The warrior had to brace his hands on the instrument panel to keep from being pitched into the windshield. More slugs tore through the plane. They were so close to the ground he could see individual tree limbs, and he was about to grab the copilot's wheel to pull the plane up when Cortez came to life and did it himself.

Wind screamed, metal creaked as the amphibian leveled out mere yards above the highest trees. Cortez cut to the right, then to the left. Their pursuer stayed glued to their tail, firing without letup.

"I can't lose him!" Cortez cried.

"Keep trying!"

They shot out over the Sucuriú and Cortez turned upriver, bringing the amphibian down low over the water.

"You've got to gain altitude," Bolan told him. "We're sitting ducks down here."

"I'll try!"

Cortez hauled back on the wheel. At the same instant another lead firestorm blistered the aircraft. A line of slugs drilled into the pilot, and his chest exploded. His hands slipped from the wheel, and the plane started to go down.

Bolan grabbed the wheel in front of him and pulled with all his strength. But it was too late; gravity had taken over. The amphibian's tail hit the river with a bone-jarring jolt. It veered to the left, then smacked belly-down with a tremendous splash, bouncing Bolan as if he were a rag doll. The plane skipped twice, and the nose rose a few feet.

A murky wall of vegetation reared in front of the aircraft. Bolan tensed for the impact and raised both arms in front of his face. The next second the amphibian plowed into the jungle like a berserk juggernaut, the din deafening. Upending shrubs and small trees, the plane shook, jounced and swerved from side to side.

A giant araucaria tree loomed in the aircraft's path. Bolan saw it and braced himself. There was a rending crash as the right wing clipped the trunk. The plane went into a spin, smashed into another tree, then slid to a grinding stop.

Bolan was battered, bruised and sore, but he couldn't afford to sit there and take stock. The smell of gas was strong, and sparks were shooting out from under the instrument panel. Undoing the seat restraint, he spun, seized his two bags and tore at the door handle.

Smoke billowed from under the floor as the warrior kicked the door wide and leaped. He hit the ground running, heading toward a log a dozen yards away. A sizzling sound filled the air, broken by a loud popping noise.

In a running jump Bolan hurled himself behind the log and flattened. The crump of the blast made it seem as if the ground rose and fell. Hot air fanned his hair. When he rose on his elbows for a look, the amphibian was in flames.

The growl of an engine reminded the warrior of the other aircraft. It roared overhead, then circled, coming back for a slower, closer inspection.

Bolan crawled into the undergrowth. He could easily have put a few shots into the plane's fuselage as it flew by, but he wanted the pilot to believe he was dead.

The white craft circled twice more. At last, the pilot apparently satisfied there were no survivors, it banked and headed inland.

The warrior walked to the log and sat. He was stranded in the jungle, hundreds of miles from Rio, thrown on his own in one of the most hostile environments in the world.

A lesser man would have quaked at his plight. Mack Bolan accepted it and adapted. The jungle held no fear for him. Surviving would be no different than it had been in the jungles of Southeast Asia where he had proved his mettle time and again.

Throwing the duffel over one shoulder, the square pack over the other, he stood and squinted at the sun, fixing his bearings. He reckoned that the river should be to the north and hiked in that direction.

Gradually the forest came to life. Monkeys frolicked in the canopy above, birds and parrots squawked and sang. Bolan wasn't fooled by the tranquil setting. He knew the many dangers to be found so he kept alert.

It took much longer than the warrior had figured to find the Sucuriú. He had to take the survival knife from the duffel and use it to chop through random tangles of vines. Once he had to make a wide detour to avoid a swarm of red ants.

The humid air made Bolan's clothes cling to his muscular frame. On reaching the river he dropped to his knees and splashed some of the tepid water on his face. He was careful not to drink any, since a single tainted mouthful would render him too weak to lift an arm, let alone a pistol.

As the warrior got to his feet he saw something that gave him cause for concern. Imprinted in the mud nearby was a huge set of jaguar tracks, not more than

four or five hours old. The big cat was just one of the
many ferocious predators he must watch out for.

Bolan hiked to the northwest, never straying more
than a dozen yards from the riverbank. Eventually the
Sucuriú would bring him to Taguarí and Carlos Cordoba. He could only hope that Cortez had been right
about how close they were. Otherwise, he was in for a
long walk.

By evening the Executioner had traveled only another mile. He constructed a roomy shelter, using
downed limbs and huge leaves, then settled down for the
night. Before another day was up he expected to be at
Taguarí. In three or four days he would be back in Rio,
job accomplished.

That night the warrior slept undisturbed while all
around him the jungle was filled with the roars, snarls,
trills and other assorted sounds made by its countless
creatures. Only once did Bolan awaken, when he heard
a low, guttural cough just outside. He gripped the Uzi
as a large animal padded around the shelter, its heavy
breathing like the rasp of a bellows. At length it left and
he lay back down.

The next morning Bolan discovered the tracks of his
visitor, the same tracks he had seen at the riverbank.
The jaguar had gone off to the south and was no doubt
miles away.

His gear over his shoulders, the warrior resumed his
solitary journey. He had covered a few hundred yards
when he came on a tract of felled trees, forest giants
blown over by a recent storm. Cautiously he picked his
way among them, constantly on the lookout for poisonous jungle vipers.

Suddenly Bolan heard voices. Crouching against one
of the downed trees, he stared at the river and saw a ca-

noe containing three bronzed Indians. They were headed downstream, away from Taguarí, and their canoe was loaded with goods they had to have received in trade. The three men were paddling strongly and soon were out of sight.

Bolan put a hand on the tree and stood. If Cordoba was on friendly terms with the neighboring tribes, he would do well to avoid contact with them.

The warrior gripped a branch so he could climb up and over and be on his way. A rumbling growl riveted him in place. Looking to his left, he saw an enormous tawny cat, the same animal that had undoubtedly visited him the night before. Its tracks had proved misleading.

The beast perched on the tree wasn't a jaguar. It was known to the natives as a *sucuarana*. The English word for it was puma.

And as Bolan stared, the puma coiled its legs, bared its fangs and inched toward him.

10

Mack Bolan remembered hearing somewhere that pumas rarely attacked people. Unless cornered, they would go out of their way to avoid contact. So instead of triggering the Uzi, he stood stock-still. He knew he could put a dozen slugs into the cat before it reached him, yet all it would take was a single slash of its razor paws to do him severe harm. He'd rather it just ran off and left him alone.

The puma crept nearer, its tail twitching madly. Just when it seemed on the verge of springing, it suddenly cocked its head skyward, listened a moment, then whirled and bounded into the foliage.

Seconds later he heard the rotors of an approaching helicopter. Whirling, he raced toward the river, barreling into a thicket and sinking to one knee as the tops of the nearby trees were buffeted by rotor wash.

A great shadow spread across the ground. Shifting, Bolan peered up through the branches and saw a small chopper painted in camouflage green and brown. It appeared to be a variation on the McDonnell Douglas 300 and was equipped with two missile-launch tubes and a nose-mounted launch sight.

As Bolan watched, the copter swung to the south. He saw no military insignia, which was all the proof he needed that the chopper belonged to Carlos Cordoba and that the arms lord had sent men to check the wreckage of the amphibian. Once they did, they might conduct a grid sweep of the area, just to be sure there were no survivors.

Turning, the warrior hurried to the river. He had to get out of there, and the fastest route was by water. He ran the risk of running into Indians, but it couldn't be helped.

Bolan didn't have to look very hard to find a suitable means of travel. Straddling a log, a long pole in his hands, he shoved off and headed upriver. The water close to shore was shallow, and by poling with a steady, powerful sweep, he was able to make good time.

He stayed near the bank so that cover was handy if he needed it. With the chopper gone the jungle was quiet. He heard the drone of insects, the croak of frogs.

A bend appeared. Bolan moved farther into the river to get past a low-hanging tree, and as he did a canoe swept around the bend toward him. There was no chance to hide. He counted three dark-haired Indians, saw the surprise on their faces. Ignoring them, he poled calmly by and resisted an urge to glance over a shoulder after they passed. Once he was beyond the bend he poled with renewed vigor.

The river widened and became more shallow near the shore, so the Executioner had to keep farther out to avoid rubbing the bottom. For more than fifteen minutes he forged steadily onward. No more Indians appeared but he did see a large snake swimming toward the log and he pulled his legs out of the water until he had outdistanced it.

A column of smoke materialized in the distance, and Bolan wondered if it could be Taguarí. Suddenly the jungle echoed with the sound of an oncoming chopper.

He steered toward shore, digging the pole into the soft bottom, his shoulder muscles rippling. The log grounded on a gravel bar a few feet from the bank, so he tossed the pole down and ran.

Bolan was almost to the brush when his right foot slipped. As he regained his footing the copter zoomed out over the river, rotated abruptly and hovered fifty feet off.

The pilot had spotted him.

Two steps and Bolan reached the undergrowth. He plunged in and heard the chopper closing fast. Darting behind a tree, he crouched as the whirlybird poised directly above him. The door on the off side had opened, and a man leaned out, an assault rifle tucked to his shoulder.

The warrior broke and ran, zigging and zagging as best he was able with the weight of the two bags slowing him down. The assault rifle cut loose, the rounds chewing up the earth at his heels. He came to a gully and flung himself across it, into dense cover.

The chopper abruptly broke off and flew back over the river. Bolan couldn't understand why they had given up until he heard a high-pitched whine and saw a green speedboat race into view, and it carried a dozen gunners. The craft looped once under the chopper, then sped to the gravel bar.

The warrior had a fight on his hands. He knew he couldn't hold his own burdened with his gear. Looking around, he saw a tree stump a few yards off. A check showed the inside was hollow, littered with chunks of dead wood. It took half a minute to scoop out a hiding place for the duffel and the pack and to cover them both. Then he turned westward and headed out.

The delay had proved costly. The gunners had already jumped from the speedboat and were fanning out as they converged. One man wore a headset, meaning he had a com link to the chopper and could be guided by the pilot.

So far they hadn't seen Bolan. He could have slipped away, but they were approaching the gully and once across might stumble on the stump. To divert them he stopped, sighted on the nearest hardman, and when he was sure, cored the man's brain.

The burst brought immediate response. Every last gunner returned fire, forcing Bolan prone, and from the river came the chopper, the guy with the assault rifle bent far out the door, searching for a target.

Bolan slanted the Uzi upward and shot at the horizontal stabilizer and tail rotor. His bullets spanged off the tail pylon, alerting the pilot, who instantly swooped out of range.

Meanwhile the gunners were coming on fast. The warrior let the business end of the Uzi slow them down, then he rose and sprinted deeper into the jungle. Now all he had to do was stay ahead of them and evade the chopper at the same time.

The copter streaked back on a strafing run, the gunner peppering the vegetation. He was firing blind, but he was no less deadly.

Bolan sought the sanctuary of a tree as bullets ate into the earth all around. The chopper flashed overhead and the warrior pivoted, sighted and put a half-dozen rounds into the gunner's back.

Arms flung wide, the body plummeted from the open door, crashing through the canopy in a spectacular whirl of limbs, both human and wooden.

The gunners from the boat pinpointed the warrior's position and joined the fray with a vengeance. Bolan raced into the forest as branches and leaves on either side crackled and snapped. He soon pulled far enough ahead that they ceased firing, but he could hear them barging through the brush in his wake. They were sacrificing stealth for speed, showing their determination to nail him at all costs.

He had anticipated as much. Carlos Cordoba had to be furious at being thwarted time and again. The word would be out to all of his operatives to nail Bolan no matter what. Perhaps there was even a bounty on his head. A hefty reward worked wonders at making marksmen out of mediocre killers.

Unexpectedly the jungle thinned and Bolan was able to move at a brisker clip. An overeager gunner sent a burst over his head so he darted to the right, putting a tree between them. He didn't waste ammo returning fire. He'd need all he had if they cornered him.

The chopper hovered off to the south so the pilot could keep Bolan in sight and relay directions to the gunners.

Without warning, the warrior came to a drop-off. He halted at the edge of the forty-foot cliff and glanced both ways. To his right the drop-off extended for dozens of yards; to his left rose an outcrop.

Bolan would make his stand there. He had done enough running. It was time to go on the offensive.

Spinning, Bolan fired several rounds at the copter to rid himself of aerial scrutiny, causing the pilot to bank and fly to the southeast. The warrior kicked at the dirt rim, dislodging chunks that cascaded over the edge. Then he dashed behind the outcrop, held the Uzi close to his chest and listened to the thud of heavy boots as the gunners drew near.

A pair of hardmen were the first to reach the drop-off. They saw where part of the rim had broken off, and assuming the warrior had gone over the side, they scanned the ground below while shouting for their comrades.

The rest of the gunners converged from several different directions. They clustered at the rim, hunching low so no one could pick them off from below.

The ruse had worked like a charm. Bolan popped up and triggered the mini-Uzi, which had been set on full-auto. Firing at a rate of twelve hundred rounds per minute, the entire magazine was emptied in seconds, spraying death in a tight arc. The gunners were caught flat-footed, their bodies perforated multiple times, jerking and twitching under the impacts. In moments they were scattered on the grass, dead or dying.

Bolan slapped in a new magazine, switched to semi-auto and approached the cliff. One of the gunners tried to lift his weapon, but Bolan saved him the trouble by firing a round into his chest.

Cordoba's killers had carried an eclectic mix of weapons. There were two Uzis, a Swedish Madsen, a Czech Skorpion and three H&K MP-5s.

The warrior confiscated one of the Uzis and all the spare magazines he could carry. Turning his steps eastward, he headed for the stump. The chopper could be heard in the distance. It circled around to the drop-off, hovered awhile, then sailed to the northwest.

It would be a while before they tried that stunt again, Bolan reflected. He had bought himself a little time. Not much, but perhaps enough to enable him to penetrate Taguarí and dispose of the Vulture.

The duffel and pack were right where Bolan had left them. He added the extra Uzi and magazines to his collection, hefted both bags over his shoulders and walked to the river.

The speedboat was long gone. Far off the column of smoke still rose. The warrior walked along the shore where he could keep one eye out for watercraft and another on the sky for aircraft.

Bolan traveled close to a mile without incident. When he was abreast of the smoke he entered the jungle to learn the cause. Soon he heard the thunk of an ax biting into wood and the yipping of a small dog.

A crude shack appeared. Beyond it a scrawny, bare-chested Brazilian was chopping down a tree, one of many he had previously felled. Near him stood a short woman dressed in a faded dress and blouse.

More than an acre had been cleared so far. Bolan figured the people were farmers, hardy souls who eked out a living by tilling the soil until they had depleted its nutrients and then moved on to start over elsewhere.

Convinced they were no threat, Bolan straightened to slip off and involuntarily started when a frenzied yipping broke out almost at his feet. A small mongrel, a puppy at that, barked and snapped at his ankles with a fury that would have done a Doberman justice.

"Go away!" Bolan growled, motioning for the pup to leave. As he did, he saw someone standing in deep shadow at the side of the house. Instinctively he brought the SMG to bear. "Come out where I can see you."

A slender figure stepped into the open, a young woman wearing a homespun dress that clung to her lithe body. She showed no fear as she walked over and picked up the pup. "Do not harm my dog," she said in accented English. "He is just protecting our home." Her flashing eyes narrowed, and she gave the warrior a probing look. "You do not have the look of one of Cordoba's killers."

"I'm not," Bolan responded.

"But that gun. What is your business here?"

"Just tell me how close I am to Taguarí and I'll go."

"You do not know?"

"I wouldn't have asked if I did." Bolan let the Uzi fall to his side so she wouldn't feel threatened.

"Taguarí is two kilometers to the northwest."

"Thanks." Bolan turned to go.

"Wait," she said. "Who are you that you do not know where you are? What is your name? What are you doing here?"

"I have business in Taguarí" was all Bolan would say. Nodding, he walked off but hadn't gone more than two steps when she was beside him, a warm hand on his elbow.

"Please do not go."

"Why not?"

"We should talk."

"About what?"

"Taguarí," the woman replied, and went swiftly on as if afraid he would leave despite her plea. "I was in town last night. I heard talk. A plane was shot down. A plane bringing a man who is no friend of Carlos Cordoba's." She paused. "Is that man you?"

Bolan wasn't about to disclose a thing to a woman he didn't know. He had no idea how trustworthy she was, what her motives for prying might be. "I really have to go."

"Please, hear me out!" she said, hanging on to his arm. "My name is Carlotta Guajardo. I live here with my father and mother. I—'' She hesitated, uncertainty twisting her lovely face.

"There's no need to tell me all this," Bolan said, prying her fingers lose.

"I hate Cordoba."

The simple statement was uttered with such force and spite that Bolan released her hand and studied her features. "Why tell me?"

"I am taking a big chance, I know, but if you are who I think you are, then you can use my help."

"Thanks, but no thanks." Bolan said. This was all too sudden for him. For all he knew, Cordoba might have had his men spread the word about him to the local farmers. Maybe a reward had been offered for anyone who turned him in.

"Please," Carlotta begged. "This is—" She broke off as an odd horn sounded a single dull note. "Our neighbor is warning us! They come!"

"Who?"

"Cordoba's pigs." Carlotta began to pull on his wrist. "We must hurry. There is a hiding place."

"I'm safer in the jungle."

"No! No! Trust me, please."

The warrior saw the older man and woman hastening toward them. Neither said a word as they halted next to a pile of branches situated close to the house, and grabbed hold. They lifted, and to Bolan's surprise the entire pile rose off the ground in one piece, revealing a large hole underneath.

"Come. Hurry."

The warrior saw that the branches were bound together so cleverly no one would notice without a close inspection. The hole was five feet deep, four wide. On the bottom was a blanket and a piece of bone.

"They will be here any minute," Carlotta said, sliding over the side. "Get down before they see us!"

Bolan looked at the couple, both of whom smiled, then eased in next to the young woman. It was a tight fit with the duffel on his back. Carlotta had given the bone to the puppy, and it was chewing heartily at their feet.

"We must be very quiet."

The man and woman carefully set the cover back in place. Enough light filtered through the branches so Bolan could dimly see Carlotta and the mongrel. He raised one of the bottom branches a fraction and saw the couple moving off to resume cutting. The man had just picked up the ax when figures appeared in the forest, a line of men armed to the teeth.

"Rivas!" Carlotta breathed.

Bolan had seen the hardman, too. Now wearing a plain khaki uniform instead of an expensive suit, Rivas strolled into the clearing and gestured. Immediately the couple was surrounded by twenty gunners, but neither seemed to care. They went about their business, the man wielding the ax with precision.

Rivas advanced and barked words at the man, who answered while chopping. Rivas frowned, tore the ax from the farmer's grasp and slapped him across the cheek. The man boldly stood his ground, answering politely when spoken to.

Bolan couldn't hear their conversation, but he knew Rivas was grilling the farmer about him. One word was all it would take. Bolan would be hopelessly trapped.

"Rivas is one of the worst of them," Carlotta whispered in the warrior's ear. "If he kills my parents, I will climb out and rip his eyes from his head with my bare hands!"

Some of the gunners were snooping around the shack. One had brazenly entered, and Bolan heard a loud crash. The puppy growled at the noise.

"Keep him quiet," Bolan warned.

The gunner ambled out of the house with half a loaf of bread in his hand. He gave a piece to another man, and they idly walked toward the hole, chewing hungrily.

Bolan placed the Uzi muzzle on the rim. "If they find us," he whispered, "I'll try to lure them off so you and your parents can escape."

"You would sacrifice yourself for us?"

The gunners were now too close for comfort. Bolan kept quiet, wishing there was a step or a toehold so he could vault out of the hole on a moment's notice if he had to, instead of having to climb out.

Suddenly there was a distinct crunching sound. Bolan looked down to see the puppy cracking the bone in its teeth.

One of the gunners stopped eating his bread, glanced up and spoke.

Carlotta swooped her pet into her arms. Not knowing Bolan had caught the pertinent words, she translated in a whisper. "He asked if the other man heard a noise." Then she kept on translating.

"I swear I heard something."

"Probably a damn bird or some animal. God, how I hate this rotten hellhole! Give me Rio or Brasília any day."

"If you hate it so much, why do you stay on?"

"For the same reason you do. The money."

Bolan was relieved when the pair walked off. He couldn't relax yet, though, because Rivas was nose to nose with Guajardo, his finger jabbing the farmer's chest. Shoving Guajardo aside, Rivas stormed into the jungle, his men dutifully following.

The warrior expected the farmer to hurry over to the hole, but Guajardo did no such thing. Instead he picked up the ax and resumed chopping. His wife remained at his side. Puzzled, Bolan gazed eastward and discovered the reason. One of the gunners was hiding behind a tree, spying on them.

"Those vermin are so predictable," Carlotta whispered. "They do the same thing every time." She nodded at the skulker. "He will stay a short while, then leave when he believes my parents have nothing to hide."

"So we're stuck here awhile."

"You do not sound happy at the idea."

"I don't like being hemmed in like this with a small army on my trail."

"You are as safe here as you would be anywhere else. Safer, since they will be busy searching the jungle."

"I owe you," Bolan said.

"Not true. If you are the man who is after Cordoba, then I am the one who owes you, and I will do all I can to help."

"I gather you want him put out of business."

"I want him dead," Carlotta declared with passion. "I want to know the worms have eaten his body and he will never hurt anyone ever again."

"What can you tell me about him and his operation?"

Carlotta leaned back, her features clouded in shadow. "He is the devil in human form. Until Cordoba came here, Taguarí was a quiet town. This whole region was peaceful. A woman did not have to fear being out alone after dark."

"What else?" Bolan prodded when she fell silent.

"There was once a church in Taguarí, and the priest had a school for the children. That is where I learned your language, helping him. He was a very wise, learned man." Her voice lowered. "Then Cordoba arrived with his jeeps and trucks and men, and before long he had driven the priest off."

"He's taken over the town?"

"From top to bottom. His men are always there, always keeping an eye on things. No one can move without them knowing. Often they get drunk and cause much trouble. Decent people take their lives into their hands when they go into Taguarí."

"Why does your family stay? Why not go somewhere else?"

"We are poor, *senhor*. We do not have animals to haul our few goods, so we would have to take a boat downriver. Cordoba controls the boats and he only lets his own people leave."

"I can see why you hate him," Bolan commented.

"No, you do not."

"What else has he done?"

"He brought Rivas here."

"I saw how Rivas treated your father. Has he been giving your family a hard time?"

"If only that was all he had done!" Carlotta said sadly. "Hector Rivas raped me."

11

The story Carlotta told was one of stark terror for the poverty-stricken people of the region. Carlos Cordoba's private army of gunners had swept into Taguarí like Nazi storm troopers, taking over the town in a single morning. From that day on, the townsmen and farmers had been subject to the arms dealer's tyranny.

Those who complained were dragged from their homes in the middle of the night and brutally beaten. Those who openly talked of reporting Cordoba to the authorities disappeared. Contact with the outside world was limited.

Not that there had ever been much to begin with. Taguarí was so remote it had lacked telephone service and electricity. Cordoba had changed all that, bringing in his own generators. But only his people had access to the new services. For everyone else it was life as usual, with one main difference. Their lives were now in the cruel hands of the arms czar.

Only the Indians were spared. Cordoba treated them royally, and in return they served as his eyes and ears in the jungle and along the river. Anything unusual was reported to him at once.

The more Bolan learned, the more he realized the mission was no ordinary hard probe. He was up against a ruthless mastermind who had a virtual lock on fifty square miles of Brazilian real estate. The odds were so stacked against him, he would have been grateful for the assistance of Phoenix Force.

But that was wishful thinking, and Bolan had to deal with reality. Yes, the forces arrayed against him seemed overwhelming. But enemies were like chains—they were only as strong as their weakest links. And Carlos Cordoba had several.

First and foremost was the arms dealer himself. If Bolan could put the man out of commission, the whole arms network might fall apart. Cordoba was the linchpin holding it all together. He was the one with the important contacts, the one with enough clout to keep his operation secret.

Second, there were the gunners. Bolan couldn't deny he was vastly outnumbered. Yet the quality of the opposition counted more than its quantity. These were ordinary criminals, hoodlums with guns, not highly trained military men. The Executioner had the edge there, and he aimed to exploit it for all it was worth.

THAT EVENING, after Bolan had shared the family's meager supper, he walked outside to the hole and hopped down. His gear was stored there on the off chance some of Cordoba's men might show. Thankfully there had been no sign of them since Rivas and company left.

Carlotta slid out of the darkness and gazed at him as he opened the duffel. "I wish you would change your mind."

"This is my fight, not yours."

"I know the area better than you. I can get you into town without being caught."

"You've given me directions. That's all I need."

"Are all Americans so stubborn?"

Bolan was filling his pockets with specific items he would need.

"Maybe you would be smarter to go back down the river," Carlotta suggested. "If anyone can reach Rio, it is you. Tell them what is happening. They will send soldiers to deal with Cordoba."

"No can do."

"Why not?"

The warrior glanced up. "Do you know what an octopus is?"

"The creature that lives in the ocean, with all the arms?"

"That's the one," Bolan said. "This Cordoba is like an octopus. His arms, his tentacles, reach out all over the world. At one time or another he's sold weapons to every terrorist organization there is. Thousands of good people have died because of him. Men, women, children." He lifted a grenade. "Different governments have tried to stop him. They cut off a tentacle here or another there, but they have never been able to get the head of the octopus. No one has ever been this close before." The grenade went into a pocket. "I'm going to see that the octopus dies."

Carlotta crouched. "Those are the most words you have spoken at any one time since I met you, and I could tell they came from the heart."

"Then you know why I must go on alone."

"Yes. But I still think you are making a mistake."

The warrior finished and climbed from the hole. He was armed with two Uzis and carried four spare magazines for each. As well, he had two pounds of C-4 plastique and accessories.

"Do not worry about your belongings," Carlotta said. "I will take care of them until you return."

"I'm grateful." Bolan touched her wrist, then jogged into the night.

The positions of the stars enabled the warrior to fix his position with as much accuracy as if he had a compass. He swung to the southwest, away from the Sucuriú. Carlotta had told him the river was patrolled at night by speedboats with spotlights, so that route was out.

Bolan planned to approach the town from the densest tract of jungle that bordered it. He moved easily over the rough terrain, while in the distance jaguars coughed and night birds screeched. Occasionally the nearby vegetation would rustle with the passage of a large animal, but none of them bothered him.

Once a loud racket broke out a hundred yards to Bolan's rear, and he stopped to listen. Something was snarling and thrashing. In a bit the noise stopped so he went on.

Soon the landmark the big man had been looking for rose in front of him. It was a hill, and from the top he could see the lights of Taguarí, just as Carlotta had told him would be the case. Prone in the grass, he studied the layout.

A few crude docks edged the river. Most of the structures were frame shanties. The hub of social activity, the bar, was the only substantial building other than a newly constructed barracks for Cordoba's men. A big fuel tank behind it resembled a gigantic mushroom. Several vehicles had been parked close to the tank, and the helicopter rested on a landing pad.

The Executioner had been disappointed to learn that Cordoba's own residence was farther up river. Taguarí was no more than a staging area and supply point, and a place where the gunners could relax, have a few drinks and buy the services of women imported by their boss to meet their needs.

Some men, though, were never satisfied. Local women had become prime targets, many being molested or raped as Carlotta had been.

That would soon stop, Bolan reflected. He quietly worked down the hill into the trees and advanced with an Uzi tucked to his ribs. According to Carlotta, there were no trip wires or magic-eye alarms ringing the town, but he couldn't take her information for granted. He was constantly on the lookout for both.

Thirty yards from the outskirts Bolan went to ground. He spotted a pair of figures walking from west to east and heard low talk. Drawing the Viper, he waited until they passed, then he catfooted in their wake, as silent as the shadows into which he blended so well.

The pair were hardmen, guards on patrol. Their conversation had to do with a certain woman at the bar who had short-changed one of them. The man intended to take the money out of her hide.

Bolan matched their pace, slowing when they did, stopping when they stopped. At length they came to a log and one of them sat to adjust his boot. The other pulled out a pack of cigarettes and tried to light one, but the breeze blew out his match so he turned his back to the log to try again.

The Executioner pounced, one arm snaking around the throat of the gunner on the log to choke off any sounds the man might make just as he speared the Viper into the man's back, then twisted the blade and ripped upward. The gunner collapsed, and Bolan jumped over the log.

In the act of touching a match to his cigarette, the second hardman glanced around. On seeing the warrior he spun, bringing up a Sten.

The Executioner beat him by a hair. The knife sliced above the Sten and into the gunner's chest. Grunting, the man took a single step backward, then fell to the ground.

Bolan dragged both bodies into the brush and frisked them. Other than the Sten and a Walther MPL, the pair had carried no weapons. Since the warrior already had the two Uzis, he didn't bother taking either of the subguns, although he did pocket some of the 9 mm ammo. He also took the matches.

He saw no one else until he was at the outskirts of Taguarí. Concealed behind high weeds Bolan saw men and women moving about on the dusty street. The former far outnumbered the latter. He spotted a jeep parked between the bar and a house and, of all things, a motor scooter by the barracks.

Carlotta had told Bolan that Cordoba seldom went to town of late, which was too bad since Bolan wanted to end it then and there. He spied an antenna on top of the barracks and made that one of his first priorities.

Music blared from the bar as Bolan crept to the side of a shanty and squatted at the rear corner. There was no activity behind the buildings, but the darkness could be deceiving. He probed every shadow carefully.

When Bolan was confident he had the back street to himself, he padded forward. He was abreast of the third shanty when drunken laughter warned him someone was approaching. An empty, rusted oil drum offered concealment, and he had just crouched down when a man and woman walked around a shanty a dozen feet away and stopped to kiss.

Bolan had to hand it to Cordoba. The arms czar was smart enough to know that the kind of men he hired would grow restless and irritable if not allowed certain amusements. He had provided them, but had done so at a distance from his home so as not to interfere with the heart of his operation. Security there was bound to be much tighter, and the gunners would always be on their toes.

The couple broke apart and the man gave the woman a few bills. Arms linked, they ambled off into the trees to transact their business arrangement.

Bolan was set to rise when something else materialized, a four-legged animal moving in his direction. It was a dog, its nose to the ground, sniffing loudly.

The warrior had the suppressed mini-Uzi on semiauto. A single stroke of the trigger and the animal would die. But he held his fire, hoping the dog would venture elsewhere, and his wish was granted.

A merry shout on the main street drew the animal's interest, and it trotted into an alley.

The Executioner rose and headed toward the fuel tank. He had to swing wide of the barracks, where a number of gunners stood outside shooting the breeze. Exercising stealth, sticking to the darker areas, he came up on the tank from the rear. No guards had been posted, but there was a high chain-link fence topped by strands of barbed wire, and a locked gate. Several fuel cans stood inside the fence lined in a tidy row.

How convenient, Bolan mused. He placed the Uzis on the ground, then stripped off the poncho and draped it over his shoulder. Climbing the fence posed no problem, and once under the barbed wire he flipped the poncho up so that the garment draped over the three spiked strands. Gingerly he climbed up and over and dropped lightly to the bare earth.

Three of the fuel cans were already full. Bolan lugged one up the fence and used to it weigh down the barbed wire as he slid over the poncho. He made the trip three more times.

The gunners thirty yards away joked and laughed, without a care in the world.

Bolan needed a fourth can. He didn't have enough plastique to go around and was going to substitute gas for explosives. So he made one last trip over the wire, claimed one of the empties and knelt in front of the spigot.

Suddenly footsteps sounded, growing louder.

The warrior flattened and crawled to the side of the tank, taking the empty with him. He saw two men approaching, one a slovenly sort swinging a ring of keys in his left hand.

"—use too damn much fuel," the man with the keys was saying. "If you ask me, the tank should have been placed closer to the river."

"I'll be sure to pass on your idea to Carlos the next time I see him."

"Go to hell, Manuel," Key Ring said. "You're not the one who has to interrupt whatever he is doing every time one of you speedboat jockeys runs low on fuel."

"Quit your griping. You're paid more as fuel-dump manager, aren't you?"

"All I got for taking this job was a fancy title and a lot of headaches."

Bolan gripped the .45 as Key Ring opened the lock and gave the gate a push.

"Will one can do for the rest of your shift?"

"Better make it two. We're out every spare minute hunting for that stinking assassin."

"What's the story there?" Key Ring asked as he picked up a can and stepped to the tank. "Is he really an American as everyone says?"

"That's the word from the top, although don't ask me how they know."

"One man against all of us. He doesn't stand a prayer."

"You wouldn't think so. But I've heard that he killed Garza, and Cortez is dead because of him, too."

"I liked Cortez. The man could drink anyone under the table."

"That's not all. It is said that Carlos is furious because the police in Rio have found the warehouse. He believes this American is to blame."

"Let us hope they find him soon."

Bolan heard the gate close and the lock snap shut. He crawled forward until he could see the pair, and when they were out of sight he went to the spigot and quickly filled the can.

Once more he scaled the fence, then had to climb back up to retrieve the poncho. He was slipping it on when a sharp click to his rear froze him where he stood.

"Not a move, American, or you die."

Out of the night walked Key Ring, a pistol clutched in his pudgy hand. "You will turn and raise your arms above your head."

Bolan had no other recourse but to obey.

"I knew there were cans missing," Key Ring said as he advanced. "It hit me as I was walking off."

"Smart man," Bolan said.

"Who would have thought I would be the one? My wallet will soon be much thicker thanks to you."

The warrior tensed. He couldn't allow the gunner to make him a prisoner. But the Uzis were lying in the grass at his feet, out of reach, and he didn't dare to try to reach under the poncho for a pistol.

"Let us see what you are carrying," Key Ring said, reaching out to pat the warrior under the left arm. He did the same under the right. "My, my. You like guns." The Para-Ordnance was pulled from its shoulder holster.

Bolan saw the hardman glance at the .45 and seized the moment. His left hand chopped hard at the gunner's wrist, causing Key Ring to drop the cocked pistol. At the same time his right hand, fingers formed in a rigid peak, speared into the hardman's jugular.

The gunner gurgled and staggered backward. In a fluid motion Bolan bent, snatched the mini-Uzi and sent three shots through the man's torso.

Turning, the warrior scanned the barracks. None of the others had heard. He picked up the .45, then slung the Uzis over his shoulders. It was time to give Carlos Cordoba even more cause to want him dead.

All the gunners were at the front of the barracks, so Bolan was able to reach the back of the building without being seen. Once there he placed a pound of C-4, unwound a short amount of detonation cord and rigged a timer to set off the fireworks electrically.

From the barracks Bolan went to the docks. Under the middle jetty he set the other pound of plastique, timed to go off half an hour after the first charge.

Next Bolan returned to the fuel tank, took a can of gas and hastened to the rear of the bar. He removed the cap so he could pour gasoline all along the base of the building and splash it on the wall. Backing up with the can tilted, the warrior left a trail of gas from the barracks to the jungle flanking the fuel tank.

The other three cans were used in a similar fashion.

By 11:50 p.m. the big man was in position. He made himself comfortable, and eventually heard the rumble of a speedboat out on the river. Shortly thereafter two men appeared at the gate to the tank.

"Santos! Where are you? We need fuel."

The pair consulted, then headed for the barracks.

Bolan removed the pack of matches from his pocket and set them in front of him. Despite the late hour Taguarí was still lively. He'd hoped all the gunners would be back in the barracks by midnight, but that appeared unlikely.

In due course the two speedboat men came back. One of them angrily tugged at the gate and the lock. They had no idea the object of their wrath was lying lifeless fifty feet away. Cursing Santos, they stormed toward the bar.

At two minutes to midnight the warrior unslung the Uzis and laid them within easy reach. He opened the matchbox, and took out a match.

One minute later he rose onto one knee.

Finally, exactly on time, the plastique attached to the barracks went off with an ear-shattering explosion that lighted up the night, blowing the rear of the building to smithereens and buckling the rest. Shouts erupted, mingled with screams. Heedless of both, Bolan lighted the match and touched the flame to a spot in front of him where the separate gas trails converged.

Fire leaped up and raced off in four different directions with a speed no man could match. Bolan pulled the grenade, yanked the pin and tossed it over the fence.

Grabbing both Uzis, he whirled and ran, counting down in his head. On the count of five he hit the dirt.

The barracks blast had been stupendous. The fuel tank going up was the Fourth of July magnified a thousand times.

A gust of dragon's breath fanned Bolan's hair and bent the trees all around him. As the gust died, he jumped up and raced to the south in a half circle that soon brought him to the edge of town.

The barracks and the bar were burning. So was a building where the prostitutes took their johns. Smoke billowed from the ruins of the fuel tank. Panic reigned in the streets. Gunners milled frantically while desperate townspeople sought to save their houses.

Mack Bolan had only just begun. Rising, an Uzi in each hand, he stalked into the midst of the bedlam. A gunner loomed in the smoke and the warrior shot him dead. Another appeared, running toward the river. He never reached it.

The Executioner was like a wolf let loose in a pigeon coop. Bolan picked off hardmen right and left. Always on the go, using the clouds of smoke to screen his movements, he stalked the streets of Taguarí, reducing Cordoba's private army a man at a time.

All went well until Bolan rounded the corner of a shanty that wasn't burning and there in front of him stood three gunners. A bearded killer with more brains than most took one look and brought up a Skorpion.

Bolan ducked back behind the shanty as rounds punched through the flimsy planks, nearly taking off his arm. He dashed across a street and plunged into a smoke cloud, holding his breath against the acrid fumes. He dropped to his belly as the Skorpion chattered again, lacing the smoke above him with lead.

Twisting, he spied three sets of ankles jogging toward him and emptied one of his Uzis, mowing them down.

Bolan had only one full magazine left, plus half a clip in the mini-Uzi. He left the empty one behind and headed for the jungle, for the hill to the south. From its crest he stood and watched Taguarí burn. He hadn't intended for the shanties to catch on fire, but many of them had.

Taguarí was in its death throes. Fully half the town was being ravaged by the flames. Most of the inhabitants had fled to the river. The townspeople were gathered to the west of the docks, the gunners on the docks themselves. Two speedboats were there and a third raced northward, drawn by the inferno.

The Executioner checked his watch. It was one minute until half-past the hour. He watched the third speedboat slow and cruise close to the jetty. From that distance he couldn't count the hardmen cramming the docks, but it was safe to say there were more than two dozen.

The second blast of plastique lighted up the northern sky. Docks, speedboats and gunners were devoured by a great, blinding light, and when the light faded and the dust thinned they were nowhere to be seen.

Thankful that things went his way, Bolan hiked toward the Guajardo farm. He would get his duffel and the other pack and begin the next phase of his plan.

THE SHACK WAS DARK when Bolan arrived. Figuring the family was asleep, he walked to the hole and stooped to remove the cover.

For Carlotta's sake, the warrior hoped that Hector Rivas had been one of those on the docks. He'd made it a point to look for Rivas but hadn't spotted him. An instant later he learned why. On lifting the cover he found himself staring at the muzzle of a Sten.

On the other end, smiling wickedly, was Hector Rivas.

12

Mack Bolan was set to let go of the cover and leap to one side when a score of armed hardmen suddenly surrounded him. Several produced flashlights.

"Please," Rivas taunted, "try something stupid so I can tell Carlos we had no choice."

The warrior simply stood there.

"I was afraid you'd be too smart for that," Rivas said. At a nod from him three men rushed up and pressed their weapons into Bolan's back. Rivas gave another nod, and a burly gunner stepped forward to give him a hand climbing out of the hole. He gave the Sten to his helper, brushed dirt from his pants and faced Bolan. "Nothing to say?"

"Been waiting long?"

"Long enough," Rivas replied. "We heard explosions in the distance. What have you done?"

"I'd rather surprise you."

Rivas grabbed the cover and threw it down. "I am going to ask Carlos for the honor of killing you myself." He took the Uzi, then gave the warrior a thorough search. The Para-Ordnance, the Tanarmi, the Targa and the knives all went into a pile. "What? No bazooka?" Rivas said. He snapped his fingers.

A gunner stepped into the light, holding the warrior's duffel, which he swiftly filled.

"Carlos will be interested in your little collection," Rivas commented. "Maybe it will give him a clue who you are."

"Don't hold your breath," Bolan said.

"Ah, yes. Speaking of which, you must be wondering about the fine family who lives here."

The warrior glanced at the house, fearing the worst. There could be only one explanation for their absence and for Rivas having been in the hole. "They had no part in this."

"Please. Don't insult my intelligence and I won't insult yours. They hid you from us. They fed you. They let you store your bag here." He grinned. "How do I know all this, you ask yourself? Because they told me. All it took was some persuasion and they talked my ears off."

"I'll bet."

Rivas chuckled and gestured. Bolan was prodded by the three gunners into following Rivas to a spot twenty yards from the shack.

"Ever hold your breath for very long?"

The strange question made the gunners laugh, but Bolan made no reply.

"Look at the ground under your feet," Rivas directed. "Tell me if you notice anything unusual."

The earth had the appearance of freshly tilled soil. Bolan stared at it, noticing large clods among the dirt, and a cold rage gripped his soul. "It's been dug up."

"I took a lesson from these dirt farmers," Rivas said. "They like to plant things so much, I did the same with them." He paused for maximum effect. "I buried them alive.

"You should have seen them fight," Rivas went on. "That old woman in particular. She scratched and clawed as we tied her, then spit out the dirt just as fast as we shoveled it on her face. It took a long time for her to die.''

All Bolan could think of was the kindly expression the woman had worn while serving him a small portion of beans.

"The old man went quietly. With dignity," Rivas continued. "Not that dignity does you much good when you're dead." He raised an arm, shouted, "Now!"

The rest of the band advanced. Bolan paid no attention until a soft sob fell on his ears. Looking up, he saw Carlotta Guajardo, her wrists bound behind her back, being prodded by a gunner with a subgun.

"Yes, I spared her," Rivas said. "Not for myself, you understand. Carlos likes to dip women even more than he does men."

"Dip?" Bolan repeated.

"You have to see it to believe it."

Carlotta went to Bolan, her eyes brimming with tears for her parents. "I am sorry," she said huskily. "We tried to resist but there were too many."

Rivas nodded at Bolan. "You have only yourself to blame. We were on our way back to Taguarí and I had a man out on point. He saw you leaving their house and followed you until he stumbled on a jaguar. The cat treed him for a few minutes, and when he could climb down you were gone."

Bolan recalled the racket he had heard in the brush. "There's one person to blame, all right," he said, and he looked straight at Rivas. "You."

"Tie him," the killer snapped.

In short order the warrior was securely bound and trailing Carlotta as the band marched toward the river.

"I'm sorry," he said softly, and received a vicious jab in the back from the gunner behind him.

At the river Rivas was handed a headset by a man bearing a radio in a backpack. Rivas slipped it on and spoke crisply into the microphone. "Vargas, this is Hector. Do you copy?" Only static greeted the question so Rivas tried again. "Vargas, answer me. How soon can the speedboats pick us up?"

One of the men had gone out to the very edge of the water. He abruptly pointed and exclaimed in Portuguese, "Mother of God! Look!"

A rosy glow framed the western sky, lending the jungle an eerie aspect, and an enormous column of smoke blotted out part of the horizon.

"What the hell is it?" Rivas barked. He swung on Bolan. "What does this mean? What have you done?"

"Go see for yourself."

Not even Bolan could have predicted the total devastation they would find. Every last building in Taguarí was either a burned-out husk or charred embers. The docks had been obliterated. All the vehicles were blackened wrecks. The heat had ignited the helicopter's fuel tanks, and the twisted wreckage was now scattered over an area the size of a city block. The bodies of Cordoba's gunners were everywhere. The townspeople were gone, vanished into the jungle, perhaps out of fear of another attack.

Rivas walked around in shock, gaping at each new sight. "How can this be?" he roared when he found his voice. Pivoting, he walked up to Bolan and seized the warrior by the front of his shirt. "Tell me!"

"Someone must have been playing with matches."

The hardman gave Bolan a shove that sent him sprawling onto the ground. "One man could not have done all this!" Rivas roared. "Who helped you?"

"Nobody."

Beside himself with fury, Rivas began to kick Bolan, trying to stave in the warrior's ribs. Bolan scrambled backward using his elbows. One kick caught him in the stomach, another in the sternum. Neither caused much pain, and the fact he was unfazed only made Rivas angrier.

Several gunners swarmed on their leader and held him back. One of them reminded Rivas that their boss wanted Bolan alive, if possible, for interrogation. Gradually Rivas calmed.

Carlotta ran to help the warrior. "Are you hurt badly?"

"Not really," he replied, as he got slowly to his feet.

"You must not make him angry again," Carlotta whispered. "There is no telling what he might do."

"I know what I'd like to do to him."

Rivas barked orders and his men bustled to set up camp. Perimeter guards were put out, and a detail was sent to sort through the debris in search of food. Later they came back with fifteen tin cans they had found in the rubble of the bar.

Bolan and Carlotta were herded close to the water and made to sit. Two gunners assumed positions close by, then ignored them.

"So we will have one more night of life, at least," Carlotta said softly.

"More if I have anything to say about it," Bolan assured her.

"They will never take their eyes off us long enough for us to escape. It is hopeless."

"There's an old saying in my country," Bolan said. "Where there's a will, there's a way." He gave her a smile. "What happened to that spunk you showed me earlier?"

"Spunk?"

"Your spirit. Your will to fight."

"It died when my parents did."

The warrior thought of his own family, dead quite a few years now as a result of Mafia manipulation, and he fell silent. Certain kinds of grief were too deep to be expressed in words, too painful to be soothed by compassion. He leaned back, rested his head on a clump of grass and pondered his next move.

The warrior knew he might be able to slip off into the river in the middle of the night if the hardmen didn't bind his feet, but he would have to leave Carlotta behind, and that he wouldn't do. She'd been through enough torment. If he could he was going to spare her from any more.

The issue was resolved later when Rivas walked over and ordered their legs tied.

Carlotta slept fitfully that night, waking Bolan now and then when she cried out softly. In the early hours of the morning she snuggled close to him for warmth, waking him yet again when her head nestled on his shoulder.

Morning brought a flurry of activity. Rivas had Taguarí checked from one end to the other for any gunners who might still be alive, but there were none. He seemed reluctant to try raising Casa Cordoba on the radio, but at midmorning did so and was told boats would be sent for them.

Bolan and Carlotta were left to themselves. She wore an expression of utter despair, and nothing Bolan said broke her gloom.

About noon the warrior heard speedboats racing down the river. He noticed that Rivas behaved nervously until the boats came into view, then the hardman put on an air of calm that evaporated when he saw one of the occupants of the lead craft.

"It's the boss!" he declared.

All the gunners became suddenly alert, standing straighter.

Bolan had no trouble picking out Carlos Cordoba from the other gunners in the boat. The arms lord had an air of authority about him; he stood at the very front, the cruel set of his mouth and the arrogant tilt of his head branding him as the sadistic tyrant he was. Cordoba was dressed in the finest clothes his illicit millions could buy. His hair had been clipped in a crew cut, and he wore a pencil-thin mustache.

There were four boats, all told. They slowed and cruised to the shore. Hardmen spilled out to flank their boss's craft, forming a living aisle down which Cordoba passed as he sauntered forward. No emotion registered on the man's face, not a hint of how he felt as he surveyed the destroyed town.

Rivas acted like he was in the presence of the Almighty. Keeping to one side of the weapons czar, he blabbed nonstop, explaining what had happened. When Cordoba turned a cold stare his way, he licked his lips and took a half step back.

At last Cordoba turned and walked up to the two prisoners. He dismissed Carlotta with a single glance, but Bolan he studied long and hard. "So you are the one who has caused me all this grief," he said at last.

"I've tried my best," the warrior responded, meeting Cordoba's flinty gaze.

"Your best was not good enough," Cordoba replied dryly. He folded his arms. "Who are you? Who do you work for?"

Bolan didn't answer.

"You will tell me, eventually. I can promise you that before I am done, you will tell me everything there is to know about your life."

"Give it your best shot," Bolan baited him.

Hector Rivas abruptly stepped up and cuffed the warrior across the face. "Speak with respect to Senhor Cordoba, you son of a bitch!" He raised his arm to strike again, then recoiled when Cordoba seized his wrist, stopping him.

"I did not say to beat him."

"But I thought—" Rivas began.

"I am very disappointed in you, Hector," Cordoba went on suavely. He let go of Rivas's sweaty wrist and wiped his hand on his pant leg. "You showed such potential at one time. What has happened to you?"

"What do you mean?" Rivas asked, his tone betraying his fright.

"You were in charge here. And now look." He waved a hand at the destruction. "Is this how you handle a situation for me?"

"But I did what you wanted. I caught this pig," Rivas said, indicating Bolan.

"At what cost?" Cordoba asked wistfully. "First the warehouse, now Taguarí."

"You can't blame the warehouse on me!"

Bolan had been listening with interest to the exchange. Clearly Cordoba tolerated no incompetence in his organization, a legacy of his army background, no doubt. It gave Bolan an idea. "Yes, he can," he interjected. When both of them glanced at him, he added, "How do you think I learned about Taguarí? I was at the warehouse and overheard Rivas mention it."

Some of the hardmen murmured, and all eyes were turned on Rivas. He blanched and blurted, "This bastard is lying just to get me in trouble. Can't you see that?"

Cordoba turned to a tall gunner who had arrived with him. "Emilio, relieve Senhor Rivas of his hardware."

"Now hold on a minute," Rivas objected, and promptly had a dozen weapons trained on him. He stood stock-still as the tall gunner disarmed him, then he was ushered to the speedboats with Bolan and Carlotta.

IN SINGLE FILE the craft sped up the river, deeper into the heart of the Mato Grosso. The jungle became denser, darker, more foreboding, the heat and humidity more oppressive.

Carlos Cordoba walked back to where Bolan and Carlotta sat. "Take a good look around you," he said to the warrior. "If you have help on the outside, you can forget them finding you. Once the Mato Grosso swallows a person, he is never seen again."

"Save your superstitious bull for the natives," Bolan responded.

"So you are familiar with the history of this territory?" Cordoba nodded. "Yes, the locals fear the Mato Grosso, and rightfully so. Few men can brave its dangers and survive, so most stay out."

"An ideal spot for your base of operations."

"Indeed. I am left to do as I please. And thanks to the marvels of modern technology, I can control my various enterprises from my own living room."

"Do your old army buddies know how you've turned out?" Bolan asked.

The arms lord frowned. "You know my background, do you? You are better informed than I would have believed possible, which confirms my suspicion that you are a government agent. But which government? The U.S.? Israel?"

Bolan made a show of admiring the lush scenery.

"You will tell me in time," Cordoba confidently predicted. "As for my army friends, most turned their backs on me when I was dishonorably discharged. The hypocrites. As if they were any less corrupt than I was." A crack appeared in the man's icy veneer, and he clenched his fists until the knuckles were white. "All I did was sell a few munitions on the side."

The revelation sparked Bolan's curiosity. Rather than ask a question that would reveal he didn't know as much as Cordoba thought he did, he said, "From military munitions to illegal arms dealer. That's a logical step, I suppose."

"You're being sarcastic. But what else could a man with my expertise do? I knew one thing—how to buy and distribute weapons. And I had made contacts that proved very rewarding after the army kicked me out."

"Especially European contacts," Bolan guessed. He had observed that a lot of the subguns and other arms used by the gunners were manufactured on the European continent or in Great Britain. The Skorpions, for instance, came from the former Czechoslovakia, the Walther MPLs from Germany, the Stens from England.

Cordoba stared intently. "Yes, you most certainly have a lot to tell me. Perhaps if you witness a dipping, it will loosen your tongue."

That made twice Bolan had heard the peculiar term. "Dipping?"

"You'll see soon enough," Cordoba said, glancing at Hector Rivas.

The river wound steadily deeper into the remote fastness of the Mato Grosso. No more settlements appeared, no farms, no isolated homesteads. Solid walls of jungle bordered the Sucuriú. Wildlife was in abundance.

From the intel Bolan had uncovered, he expected Casa Cordoba to be grand in scope. But he was unprepared for the sight of the sprawling fortress that came into view as the speedboats rounded a bend.

High white walls completely surrounded a ten-acre estate. Guard towers were situated at each corner, and an M-60 was mounted at the center of the front wall above a huge steel gate that permitted access to the palatial grounds. A satellite dish and other communications equipment perched on top of the villa's roof.

Gunners were everywhere. Guards patrolled walkways atop the walls constantly. A row of vehicles was parked alongside an immense corrugated metal structure, and outside the walls, lined up on a private airstrip, were three sleek planes.

Bolan noted the position of two fuel tanks, one near the airstrip, another near the corrugated structure. A newly painted hut at one corner had overhead wires linking it to the house and the other buildings, leading the warrior to conclude it was the generator shack.

"As you can see, I've done quite well for myself," Cordoba boasted.

"At the cost of how many lives?"

The arms lord plucked a piece of lint from his sleeve. "I do not concern myself with such trivial matters. I am a businessman providing needed merchandise, nothing more."

"You're a renegade who has to be stopped," Bolan corrected him.

"And who will topple me? You?" Cordoba chuckled. "In a day or so you will cease to exist. Within a week I will have my operation in Rio restored to full efficiency. In a year I will have recouped all my losses." He slid from the jeep as it braked in front of the villa. "So you see, you have gone to all this effort for nothing. You are no worse than a mosquito to me, and like a mosquito you will be squashed." He walked to the door, which was promptly opened by a servant. "Emilio, bring them."

The interior of the house was a shrine to limitless wealth. Pile carpet an inch thick cushioned their footsteps. Fine paintings hung on the walls.

Bolan was pushed through an arched doorway into a spacious chamber that contained a dining table capable of seating fifty. Beyond was a closed door that Cordoba shoved wide so they could enter.

The warrior didn't know what to make of the contraption before him. Three long chains dangled from a winch that was suspended from the ceiling. Under the chain, in the middle of the floor, was a marble basin three feet in diameter that contained a vile greenish-yellow liquid that reeked.

Emilio prodded Bolan and Carlotta over against a wall, then trained his weapon on them.

Seconds later Hector Rivas entered the room, wedged between two gunners. He saw the dangling chains, let out a terrified screech and attempted to pull loose. "No!" he shouted. "Not this! Not after all I have done for you!"

"Would you rather I fed you to the piranha?" Cordoba retorted. "Prepare him."

Rivas fought hard, kicking, biting and thrashing about. But it was no use. He was overpowered by five hardmen, manacles were attached to his wrists and a single large manacle was clamped around both ankles. He was hoisted off the ground, and the chains were attached to metal loops in the manacles. At the end Rivas hung upside down over the marble basin.

"Please, no! I will do anything! I will make it up to you! Just let me down!"

Cordoba stepped to the basin rim and gave Rivas a pat on the cheek. "I do so despise a coward."

"*Please,* Carlos!"

"Lower him," the arms lord commanded.

Bolan had a fair notion of what to expect. "Don't look," he cautioned Carlotta, but she was glued to the ghastly spectacle, her face pale.

Rivas screamed in terror. Tears flowed over his brow. When he was six inches above the foul brew he became rabid with panic and furiously fought the restraints, the veins on his temples bulging from his exertions. Inch by inch he dropped lower, coughing from the fumes. Just as his hair was about to sink under the surface, the winch stopped.

Carlos Cordoba leaned down and spit in Rivas's face. "Remember me in hell," he said, then straightened and grinned. "Dip him."

13

Mack Bolan tried to step in front of Carlotta to block her view, but the gunner named Emilio slammed him against the wall.

Rivas wailed as his hair touched the liquid. There was a loud hiss and gray wisps wafted upward. Then his forehead sank into the brew and he uttered a bloodcurdling shriek. He thrashed wildly, continuing to shriek until the liquid poured into his open mouth. Blubbering and spitting, he tried to pull himself out but slipped back. His whole head vanished, and his body immediately went limp.

"Stop!" Cordoba ordered. Pivoting, he regarded Bolan and the woman. "Which one of you should I pick next?"

Carlotta raised a hand to her mouth and cowered back. "What is that terrible poison?"

"You really don't know?" Cordoba rejoined. "It's not poison, my dear. It's acid. Sulfuric acid, to be precise." He reached out to touch the nearest chain. "I visited a chemical plant once during my army days and never forgot the demonstration they put on. A block of metal was dropped into a vat of acid and had been dissolved to nothing an hour later when we returned." He nudged the body. "Give our friend here another ten minutes of my concentrated treatment and his head will do the same."

"You are a fiend!" Carlotta railed.

"On the contrary, I am practical. Once his head is gone and we give his hands the same treatment, there isn't a forensics lab in the world that will be able to identify him should his body somehow turn up after we dump it in the jungle."

"You could have just shot him and buried him far away," Carlotta said. "No one would ever find the body."

"True. But this way is so much more gratifying." Cordoba strode to the doorway. "Emilio, take them to a holding cell and keep them there until I send for them. They are to receive no food, no water, nothing. Understood?"

Emilio nodded.

The arms lord beamed at them. "Enjoy your stay at Casa Cordoba." With one more look at Rivas, he left the room.

Bolan had been profoundly impressed by the demonstration, but in a way that Cordoba couldn't have foreseen. The warrior had been filled with a cold, calculated rage.

The Executioner had lost track of all the drug dealers, smugglers and illicit weapons suppliers he'd tangled with during his long battle against the forces of evil, but he had met few like Carlos Cordoba. The man was in a class by himself, the living embodiment of all that Bolan had devoted his life to fighting.

To say the man was ruthless wasn't enough. To describe him as a psychopath didn't do him justice. To point out he had criminal tendencies was a lame excuse for his behavior.

No, there was much more to Carlos Cordoba. He was a living example of all that was darkest in human nature. He was as foul as the chemical brew in which he disintegrated human heads, and, worse, he knew it and reveled in it.

Carlotta and Bolan were guided down a flight of stairs to a basement level. Doors containing barred windows lined both sides of the corridor. A pale man holding a set of keys led Emilio to a cell halfway down the hall and worked the lock.

Bolan was shoved inside first. He tripped, regained his balance and turned in time to cushion Carlotta when she was given the same rough treatment. The metal door clanged shut, and they were shrouded in gloom. Other than her heavy breathing, the cells were deathly quiet.

"Oh, God," Carlotta said softly, moving to the sole piece of furniture, a small cot. She sat and hung her head. "I can't stand the thought of dying that way."

"Then don't think about it," Bolan advised. He prowled the walls, noting a small air vent in the ceiling. There were no other openings, no windows.

"How can I help it? You saw. I will never forget that sight as long as I live."

Bolan walked to the cot. "How sharp are your teeth?"

"What?"

Turning, Bolan wagged his wrists. "Start chewing. If I hear the guard coming I'll move away and we'll act as innocent as newborns."

"You want me to chew through your ropes? That will take hours."

"Do you have something better to do?"

Carlotta gazed at the big man as if seeing him for the first time. "I have never met anyone like you, *senhor*. You never give up, do you?"

"Never."

"Then I can do no less." She bent to the ropes. "Now be still so I do not bite you by mistake."

BOLAN'S INNER CLOCK told him the time was close to four in the afternoon. The final strands of the rope parted, and he was able to confirm the hour by his watch. He rubbed both wrists to restore circulation, then quickly untied Carlotta.

"What now? We are still prisoners."

"Not for long." Bolan gathered the ropes and made one long piece out of them. Moving to the door, he peeked out the window and saw no one. He sank to one knee, swiftly looped one end of the rope around his left ankle and beckoned Carlotta.

"Why are you doing that?"

Bolan grasped her right ankle and pulled it closer so he could tie the opposite end of the rope to her. Rising, he stepped back until the rope was taut. "Just wide enough," he said.

"For what?"

"I'll show you." Bolan gripped her shoulders and positioned her to the left of the door and about a yard from it. He then stepped to the right of the door and held his hands behind his back. "Three or four of them will come for us. When they look in, keep your arms out of sight so they think we're still tied." He took a half step toward her so the slack rope was flat on the floor. "Say something to them as they enter, anything that will keep them looking at you, not down at the floor."

"Oh. I understand." Carlotta gazed skeptically at the rope. "But what good does this do? Do you plan to trip all of them?"

"Just one is all it should take," Bolan replied. "If I can grab his gun before the others put a few rounds into me, we'll have a fighting chance."

"Your idea is crazy."

"Do you have a better one?"

"No, I—" Carlotta gasped as voices sounded down the corridor. "It must be them!"

"Whatever you do, don't move," Bolan directed her. "And keep your legs as rigid as you can."

"I'm scared."

"Who wouldn't be?"

The voices came closer. Momentarily the pale jailer peered in through the window and glanced from the warrior to Carlotta. "Senhor Cordoba wants to see you," he announced.

Bolan heard the key rasp in the lock. He had positioned himself so that the door would open an inch shy of the rope. Unless the gunners were looking straight down, they wouldn't spot it.

There were three hardmen, including the jailer. True to form, Emilio, the first one to enter, glanced at the warrior and Carlotta, concentrating on them to the exclusion of all else. He had a Skorpion fitted with a 20-round box magazine in his right hand and he gestured with it as he came in. "You will—" he began.

Carlotta threw back her head and screeched at the top of her lungs, "Don't touch me!"

Emilio's natural reaction was to swing toward her, just as he was taking his second step.

Simultaneously Bolan took a stride of his own as if to go out the door. In doing so he elevated the rope just enough for it to catch on Emilio's lower leg. The unprepared gunner started to pitch forward, and in that instant Bolan slashed a knife-hand blow to Emilio's neck while at the same moment he tore the Skorpion from the gunner's grasp.

It all went so smoothly that the second hardman and the jailer had no time to get off a shot. The other hardman tried, bringing his SMG up as Emilio fell, but Emilio blocked his line of fire. Before he could compensate he was covered by the Skorpion.

"Who wants to die first?" Bolan asked.

Emilio was on his knees, a hand pressed to his throat. Beet red, he glared at the warrior, then growled over his shoulder, in Portuguese, "Shoot the son of a bitch!"

Neither of the other men seemed overly eager to test whether their reflexes were up to beating Bolan's trigger finger. The warrior knew he had to move swiftly, before they mustered their nerve or anyone else arrived on the scene. He motioned with the Skorpion. "Inside! Put down your guns!" His Portuguese was poor, but they understood.

Reluctantly the two killers complied. Bolan waved them over against the wall, then motioned for Emilio to join them.

"Untie our ankles," Bolan directed Carlotta. He pushed the door almost closed, then picked up an MPi-69 Steyr subgun that had dropped to the floor. It was Austrian-made, a 9 mm, which gave it more stopping power than the 7.65 mm Skorpion. He gave the lighter subgun to Carlotta.

The third weapon, the one the jailer had carried, was a Walther MPL. Bolan slung it over his left shoulder, then removed the keys from the lock and closed the door all the way. "Tell them to take off their shoes and socks," he instructed Carlotta.

Between the shoelaces and the rope, Bolan had enough to bind all three men while Carlotta covered them. Their socks served as gags.

Prior to leaving, Bolan removed the poncho and his shirt. In their place he substituted Emilio's shirt. Then, taking Carlotta's hand, he stepped out and locked the door behind them.

"Which way?" she wondered.

Bolan headed in the opposite direction than the one they had come, acting on the assumption they would run into fewer gunners farther from the main corridors. He had only gone a few dozen feet when he saw a grimy face staring at him from one of the cells. "Who are you?" he asked in Portuguese. The man responded in a dialect with which Bolan was unfamiliar. "Can you translate for me?" he asked Carlotta.

"Yes. He said his name is Amadeo Sandoval."

"What are you in here for?"

"I am a farmer," Carlotta translated. "I spoke out against Cordoba and he had me brought here."

"Do you know what he intends to do with you?"

"I will be dipped in acid."

Bolan gazed along the hallway. More anxious faces had appeared, one a boy no older than fifteen or sixteen. "And these?" he asked, gesturing.

"They are all guilty of angering Cordoba one way or another, and they will all share the same fate."

"How would you like a chance to fight for your lives?"

Sandoval gripped the thin bars. "Free us, and you will not be sorry."

The warrior didn't hesitate. He unlocked Sandoval's door and shoved it open, then went from cell to cell, freeing every prisoner he found. When he was done, eight men and the boy were awaiting his instructions.

"This way," Bolan said, continuing down the corridor to a stairwell. He listened but heard no footsteps. Cautiously climbing, he stopped at the next landing and cracked the door. Corridors led off in three directions. He held the door for the rest, motioning them down the left-hand branch.

The warrior had a plan, such as it was. Since they had to escape before Emilio and the others were found and an alarm was sounded, he was going to try to gain the south wall. Thanks to the arrangement of the gardens there was less open ground to cross, and once over the wall, the jungle lay only a few dozen yards off.

Bolan remembered the vehicles parked near the corrugated building and asked Carlotta to find out if any of the prisoners knew how to drive. None did.

The next door opened onto brilliant sunlight. Bolan scanned the grounds before venturing outside. Several gunners stood in front of the corrugated building, and two unarmed men by the gravel drive.

"We'll have to try a bluff," Bolan said, waiting while Carlotta informed the prisoners. "Walk out there as if you don't have a care in the world and maybe no one will pay much attention. Stay close to me. If lead starts flying, keep low and get to the metal building."

"What about me?" Carlotta asked. "They will be suspicious if they see a woman carrying a gun."

Bolan gave the Skorpion to Sandoval and briefly explained its use. Then he boldly stepped out, the MPi-69 at his side, his finger on the trigger. He saw one of the men near the corrugated building glance at them and look away. Then everything went to hell.

A Klaxon blared inside the villa. The refrain was taken up by sirens outside the house. Shouts erupted across the estate as hardmen demanded to know what was going on.

The men near the metal building headed toward the villa at double time. Bolan saw the lead man staring at his little group and was ready when the gunner raised an assault rifle. The warrior triggered the MPi-69, taking out all three hardmen with a long sustained burst. Pivoting, he dropped another gunner as the man rounded a corner of the villa.

"Hurry!" Bolan yelled, backpedaling as the prisoners raced by him.

A hefty man barreled out of the same exit they had used. He was holding a subgun, but the barrel was pointed at the grass. In the fraction of a second it took him to lift the weapon, the warrior drilled a trio of slugs through his chest.

The steel gates began to close, and Bolan saw the M-60 operator swivel the big gun around. The range was too great for his subgun but not for the M-60. He was urging the prisoners to go faster when the machine gun chattered and bullets bit chunks out of the earth near his feet.

They had to go past the vehicles, three of which were jeeps. Bolan ducked behind one and opened fire to discourage a team of hardmen closing from the northwest. Keeping the jeep between himself and the M-60, the Executioner retreated into the corrugated building and flattened against a wall.

Gunners had been racing toward the escapees from all directions. Oddly none of the hardmen had yet opened fire, except for the M-60 operator and he had already stopped.

Bolan turned to see if there was another way out and instead learned the reason none of Cordoba's men were shooting. The building was a smaller version of the warehouse in Rio, crammed with munitions crates stacked halfway to the ceiling. There was enough on hand to reduce the entire estate to rubble, and all it would take was one stray shot into just the right crate.

Carlotta and the prisoners were bravely trying not to show their fear. "What do we do?" she called out. "They have us trapped."

"Give a yell if they rush us," Bolan said. He moved among the pallets until he found a crate of Stens. With the aid of three prisoners he brought the crate up front and smashed it open. Each of the unarmed prisoners received one and a short lesson in firing techniques.

Bolan had picked the Stens for a practical reason. Due to its low cyclic rate, tapping out short burst on a Sten was easier than on most other subguns. And short bursts lent to greater accuracy.

The warrior had just taken his post near the entrance when the jarring sound of a ringing telephone drew him to a desk in the corner. He was surprised to find his duffel and pack lying on a chair beside it.

"Yeah?" Bolan said into the receiver.

"Surrender and make this easier on both of us."

"No way."

Cordoba cursed, then said, "There is only one way in and out of that building. You cannot possibly escape."

"Then open fire whenever you're ready."

Cordoba cursed again.

"Looks like we have a stalemate."

"What if I give you my word you will all be released unharmed?"

"Your word is worth squat."

"Mark my words. This will go very bad for whoever does not cooperate."

"Keep one thing in mind before you try anything."

"What?"

"I've rigged the place to blow," Bolan lied. "Attack us and you can kiss another million or two goodbye." He heard a hiss and the line went dead.

"Was that Cordoba?" Carlotta inquired.

"Yes."

"What did he want?"

"To play poker."

"I'm sorry?"

"Never mind." Bolan went to the entrance. A sizable army now had them boxed in. He could see Emilio, but not the arms lord.

Taking Carlotta along, Bolan hunted for another way out of the building. There were a few windows, too high to be reached without a boost.

Bolan had four of the men stack crates under a window on the south side, then he climbed to the sill and peered out. A single gunner squatted twenty yards away, next to a rosebush.

"We wait for sunset," the warrior said as he descended. "I'll sneak you out first, Carlotta, and come back for the rest."

"I want no special treatment," she responded.

They walked to the front and Bolan had her relay his proposal. None of the prisoners cared to be left behind, but it was agreed that all of them leaving at once would be too risky. A compromise was reached. Bolan would take out half at a time, coming back for the second group as soon as the first was safely beyond the walls.

The sun had dipped below the steamy horizon when the telephone rang again. Cordoba didn't mince words.

"Either give up right this minute, or all of you will be dipped feet-first."

"You have it backward," Bolan said. "Have your men fall back or we'll blow your munitions sky high."

"You're bluffing. You would be killed in the blast."

"At least it would be over quickly," Bolan said.

"I will give you an hour to think about it."

"Give us all night. We won't change our minds." Bolan hung up, then carried his duffel and pack over to the south window. He checked on the guard, who was now sitting on the ground.

The prisoners drew lots to see who would go first. The boy was one of the lucky ones; Carlotta and Sandoval weren't.

Bolan objected, insisting Carlotta be permitted to go. The men were willing, but the woman stubbornly refused.

"I will do what is fair and wait my turn like the rest. If it is my time to die, then I will try to do as my father did and die with dignity."

No amount of persuasion would change her mind. The sun was gone when Bolan scaled the crates again and slowly cranked the window open. Floodlights had flared to life with the advent of darkness, the majority trained on the outer wall and the maze of shrubberies in the garden. Few shone down on the warehouse, and those that did illuminated the front and the back, not the sides.

Bolan had the duffel and pack passed up to him. He eased out the window, feeling his hair fanned by a cool breeze, and leaned down as far as he could without falling. Slowly he lowered the duffel and the pack to the grass. Then, hanging by one arm, he dropped down himself.

Crouched in the shadows, Bolan drew the Viper. Once again he had a knife on each ankle, the .45 under one arm, the Tanarmi under the other. And he had traded in the MPi-69 for the suppressed mini-Uzi.

Now the big man crept across the grounds, bearing to the left so he could circle around and come up on the gunner from behind. Everything depended on him, on how silently he killed the hardman. Should he fail, Cordoba's army would swarm around the building and it would all be over.

The warrior stealthily crossed an open space to a row of tall flowers and from there moved into position to the rear of the rosebush. Pausing, he ducked low to the ground in order to spot the gunner's inky silhouette. As he did, the man suddenly materialized on his right and pointed a subgun at the warrior's head.

14

The Executioner would never know why the gunner didn't shoot him at that very instant. Maybe the man wasn't sure Bolan was an enemy, or maybe he was under a standing order to take the prisoners alive. Whatever the reason, the man pointed his submachine gun, then leaned forward so he could see the warrior's face.

Bolan whirled and threw the Viper with all the precision years of practice had given him. The blade flashed through the air, striking the gunner at the base of the throat. In the same movement the warrior stepped in close and gripped the man's gun arm, applying a lock that bent the elbow at such a drastic angle the man had no choice but to let go of his weapon.

The gunner sagged to his knees, his wide eyes pleading as he tore the Viper out and flung it from him. He opened his mouth to shout but the warrior was on him first, covering his mouth with a steely hand.

Bolan held tight as his adversary shook and gagged. Once the convulsions stopped, he set the body on the ground.

Since there was no time to lose, Bolan hurried to the south window. He called softly and the boy slipped out. One by one the other four dropped, and once they were ready Bolan slung his bags over his arms and moved rapidly into the garden.

It took longer than the warrior had counted on to reach the wall. Open spaces had to be avoided, and there were several points where floodlights forced them to flatten and crawl.

Once at the wall a new problem presented itself. Not only was it bathed in bright light, they also had no means to reach the top.

Bolan paused, debating which way to go. There had to be steps somewhere, and the most likely place would be at the front of the estate. To get there, though, they had to sneak by the hardmen gathered in front of the metal building.

What choice did they have? Bolan reflected, and headed out. With a little luck they might make it, since Cordoba's hardmen had their attention riveted on the warehouse. He hastened into the garden and moved as fast as he dared eastward.

Presently the warrior saw a flight of stairs leading to the guard tower at the southwest corner. The guards had moved closer to the machine-gun emplacement above the gate, which put the warehouse entrance in their field of fire.

Bolan didn't see how he could gain the tower without being spotted. Huddled alongside a tall bush, he gauged the distance and glanced at the others. He would have them wait while he went to get Carlotta and the rest. Together, they'd fight their way out.

But the following second a sharp command shattered the night, and a volley of automatic fire poured into the corrugated building. Bolan's pulse raced as he glided around the bush and rose high enough to see.

The gunners were aiming at the base of the corrugated wall, where there was less likelihood of a ricochet. Sparks flew as jagged holes sprouted. Carlotta and the other defenders were returning fire, but they were inexperienced and few of their rounds found targets.

Bolan wanted to help, but his options were limited. He was too far off to use the Uzi, and he would be spotted the moment he raced into the open. He reached for the duffel, his hand on the zipper when he saw several hardmen wearing gas masks dart close to the building and fire canisters inside. Tear gas.

A vile yellow cloud spewed into the interior, obscuring everything. Bolan heard commands shouted, watched the gunners quickly retreat. Frantic figures stumbled through the cloud, desperately trying to reach clear air as they wheezed and choked. All but one of the defenders collapsed after taking a few steps. The last, one of the men, broke out of the cloud, then fell to his knees. A sharp shout brought a blast of automatic fire that crumpled him in a bloody heap.

Bolan's blood ran cold. They had used poison gas, not tear gas. Cordoba had waited until dark so his men could slip in close enough to fire the canisters without being picked off. As usual, the devious devil had thought of everything. Or almost everything.

The warrior's face was an iron mask as he unzipped the duffel, shoved the Uzi in and removed the Whitworth Express. The 3-shot magazine was already inserted. He palmed a spare, closed the duffel and stood.

The prisoners couldn't hide their worry. Bolan motioned at them, then charged, bursting from the bushes at full speed. He flew up the stairs in long bounds and reached the upper wall before the guards and the M-60 gunner awoke to his presence. Once they did, it was too late. The stock flush with his shoulder, Bolan took aim.

Thunder crackled across the estate, and at the blast a guard was lifted as if by an unseen hand and thrown to the hard ground below.

At the next boom the second guard lost part of his head.

The hardman manning the M-60 attempted to turn the machine gun on its tripod.

Bolan smoothly worked the bolt on his rifle, inserting a third round into the chamber of the Express. He sighted dead-center on the gunner's chest and squeezed.

As if smashed by a battering ram, the machine gunner hurtled backward, leaving a crimson smear on the wall as he slid a dozen feet.

"Come on!" Bolan bellowed, running toward the M-60. He replaced the spent magazine on the fly and dropped a hardman standing near the gate.

Cordoba and his men had heard the rifle shots. Some were already heading for the gate, others firing recklessly since they were too far away to hit anything.

From the opposite guard tower rushed a gunner with more courage than brains. Bolan barely had to break stride to nail him. As he neared the machine gun, rounds began smacking against the wall and whizzing overhead.

It took only a moment for Bolan to slide behind the M-60 and bring it to bear on the swarm of hardmen. He paused long enough to point at the outer edge of the wall and hoped the prisoners understood. Then he hunched over the machine gun and got down to business.

The foremost ranks of hardmen were easy prey. Bolan raked them from right to left and left to right and bodies toppled like leaves in a gale. Then the main group scattered, returning fire furiously.

Bolan had to keep them pinned down long enough for the prisoners to reach safety. A withering, sustained burst served that purpose, but it also gave the hardmen the opportunity to fix a bead on him. Their shots were getting closer. One hit the M-60 and whined into the darkness, jarring the weapon in his hands.

At last the ammo belt was used up. Racing to the outer rim, the warrior slung the Whitworth, adjusted the duffel and his pack, and slid over the edge.

It was a four-foot drop to the top of the gate. Bolan clutched at the steel bars as he fell and managed to catch hold, but the jolt of stopping seared both shoulders with pain and caused him to slam against the bars so hard his teeth rattled. He hung for a moment, catching his breath, then descended rapidly.

Slugs screamed off the bars, a few nipping at Bolan's clothes. When he was six feet from the ground he let go and dropped, bending his knees to better absorb the shock. Whirling, he sped toward the jungle, as the gunners within the estate rose en masse and bore down on the gate with their weapons blazing.

All the prisoners except one were close to the jungle. The man in question limped badly and was being assisted by the boy.

The warrior poured on the speed to overtake them and lend a hand. Otherwise they would be cut down before they reached cover. A glance back revealed the maddened mass of gunners had rounded a bend in the gravel drive and were on the last straight stretch to the gate.

The boy and the injured prisoner were doing their best, but from the angle at which the man's leg was bent, it was apparent he had broken it. Bolan came alongside, slipped an arm around the man's waist and helped propel him toward the lush vegetation.

Behind them the gate was slowly opening. Automatic fire streamed between the gaps in the bars, the rounds biting into the earth on both sides of the fleeing trio.

The dark jungle was only a yard off when Bolan felt the man he was holding stiffen and heard him cry out. They gained the temporary shelter of the undergrowth as the prisoner went limp, exhaling his last breath in a strangled gasp. Bolan quickly lowered him, then gave the boy a shove. "Go!" he barked.

By now the gate was open enough to permit the hardmen to barrel through in pursuit. Bolan pulled a fragmentation grenade from his pocket and let it fly at the leading gunners. Some saw the bomb, yelled warnings and hit the dirt. Those who didn't paid for their folly with their lives.

The blast temporarily halted the rush. Bolan sprinted after the prisoners, orienting himself as he fled. He was in a strip of jungle that bordered the river. Up ahead, perhaps a hundred yards, were the docks. Off to his right the gravel road connected the docks to the villa. To his left was solid jungle that extended for limitless miles into the depths of the Mato Grosso.

He soon spotted the prisoners, who had stopped and were waiting for him. He assumed the lead without a word and kept on going. His first priority had to be to get them out of there. He couldn't take on Cordoba's small army and protect them at the same time.

Three speedboats were tied up at the docks. Bolan was puzzled at not finding any gunners present, then he realized they had to have heard the uproar at the villa and had gone to investigate. He jogged to the first boat, hopped in behind the wheel and turned the engine over.

The prisoners piled on. Bolan indicated one of them should take the controls, and an elderly man in tattered clothes did so. Hurrying onto the dock, the warrior waved them off but they hesitated, unwilling to leave him.

"Go!" the warrior ordered.

Unexpectedly the boy spoke up in halting English. "You come!"

"I have work to do," Bolan replied. "Get going. Now!"

"But—" the boy objected.

Bolan heard shouts far up the road. "There's no time! Cast off and go!"

Reluctantly the prisoners obeyed. As the boat picked up speed, Bolan hastened to the edge of the jungle and stopped. He had two grenades left, and while he would rather have saved them for later, he couldn't permit the hardmen to give chase in the remaining speedboats. He hefted both grenades, judged the distance carefully, and threw, one after the other.

A pitcher in the major leagues could not have thrown more accurately. Each grenade thudded onto a speedboat, and seconds later both boats exploded. One burst into flames and set the dock on fire.

The big man didn't linger. He darted into the underbrush and crouched as scores of enraged hardmen pounded down the road to the shore. The fleeing speedboat was spotted, and some of the gunners foolishly wasted ammo firing at it.

At last something had gone Bolan's way. The hardmen thought he was on the boat; none was making an effort to spread out and search the area. Backing away, he turned and angled to the northwest. There was one more job he had to do, and do swiftly, or the prisoners would never reach safety.

The airstrip was deserted, but Bolan knew it wouldn't be for long. Cordoba would have the planes go after the speedboat and strafe it until it sank. At the base of a high tree he knelt and opened the duffel. Two pounds of C-4 plastique were left. He saved one pound and divided the other into thirds, then went from plane to plane affixing the plastic explosive where it would do the most damage. There was barely enough det cord left to put him at a safe distance. He rigged up the detonator and was all set to reduce Cordoba's little air force to so much kindling when five gunners appeared, coming from the villa.

Bolan dropped onto his belly. One of them had to have spotted him because they opened fire, overlooking the fact subguns were designed for close-quarter use. From forty yards out all they did was spray the air. And as further proof of their incompetence, they fired long bursts, making it harder for them to control their weapons. Bolan laid still and waited.

The gunners had to pass the planes to reach him. Soon they were close to the aircraft, and their shots were coming much too close to Bolan for comfort. He tucked his cheek to the soil and set off the plastique.

Caught in the triple blast, the hardmen were bowled over by the concussion. Some lost limbs. One was literally blown apart. Another was pierced by a jagged shard the size of a spear.

Bolan lost no time fetching the duffel and his other pack. He traveled into the jungle for a quarter of a mile, then circled around and came up on the fortress from the west. The fork of a tree offered a convenient roost from which to spy on the activity taking place.

Two jeeps and eight or nine hardmen were out at the airstrip. The headlights bathed six men who shortly entered the jungle in search of the warrior.

At the villa men were busy with various tasks. Bodies were being collected. Guards were taking positions on the walls. No one, Bolan observed, went anywhere near the warehouse, which told him the poison gas hadn't yet dissipated. He saw no sign of Carlos Cordoba and assumed the arms lord was in the villa.

Next Bolan itemized his arsenal. He had the pound of C-4, the Whitworth Express and forty-four rounds of Winchester .458 ammo. There was plenty of ammunition for the mini-Uzi and the pistols, and he also had his surprise package.

A glint of moonlight on the roof of the villa drew Bolan's interest. The satellite dish was rotating on its axis, either for Cordoba to pick up a specific feed or to transmit. The warrior could make an educated guess which. It was doubtful the arms lord liked being stranded at the fortress, so at that moment Cordoba had to be getting set to contact underlings far down the river to order boats or planes to be sent right away.

Bolan wasn't going to let that happen. Setting the pack in front of him, he opened the top flap. It was fitting, he mused, that he was about to bring Cordoba's illicit empire crashing down with the very same ordnance Golden Scimitar had used on the Capitol Building in Washington, D.C.

The warrior was very familiar with the LAW rocket. Lightweight and easy to use, the M-72 A-1 had a range of three hundred yards or better, and a single rocket could take out a tank.

The tree in which Bolan sat was only twenty yards from the wall. He raised the rocket launcher, slid out the extended tube and sighted on the roof of the villa. For a few moments he was completely still. Then he pressed the firing switch and felt the rocket launcher kick.

The blast ripped the satellite dish from its moorings and catapulted it high into the air. It crashed down as twisted scrap and fell through the gaping hole that had appeared in the roof.

Panic seized the gunners. There were strident shouts. Men rushed every which way, some toward the house, some toward the walls.

The Executioner aimed his second rocket at the warehouse. He watched the rocket streak into the corrugated metal, heard the din of the explosion. Another, smaller, blast sounded moments later as smoke poured from the structure.

Bolan had hoped the LAW would trigger an explosion that would destroy the whole warehouse. He took aim again, then stabbed the black button.

This time the rocket hit the southeast corner, and for a few fleeting seconds the Brazilian night was transformed into day. A miniature sun flared to life, embracing the estate in its fiery creation. Some gunners running toward the building were the first casualties of the tremendous blast that ensued; men farther away were flattened where they stood; guards on the wall were buffeted fiercely; part of the villa buckled as if stepped on by a giant foot.

The warrior sent the fourth and fifth rockets into portions of the villa still intact. The last rocket was fired at the guard tower nearest his position, destroying it and part of the outer wall.

Thick clouds of smoke and dust choked the fortress. Gunners stumbled blindly about while others writhed in agony. More hardmen stumbled from the villa, many wounded, many hacking violently due to the smoke inhalation.

Bolan was content to sit and view the carnage. He had sounded the death knell for Casa Cordoba. Now all he had to do was terminate the man.

The warrior slung the Uzi and took the Whitworth from the duffel. He inserted a new magazine, then settled down to wait with the patience born of long experience as a seasoned sniper. Eventually the arms lord would appear, and when he did the warrior would be ready.

A few minutes had gone by when Bolan heard a faint snap, as if something or someone had stepped on a twig. Twisting, he scanned the jungle but saw nothing that would account for the sound. Then a shadow detached itself from the trunk of a tree forty feet away and flowed over the ground with uncanny swiftness. He had just a glimpse of the figure before it disappeared behind another tree, yet that glimpse was enough. It was an Indian.

Bolan shouldn't have been surprised, but he was. It made sense for Cordoba to have hired a few Indians who knew the territory well to work as guides, hunters and trackers. He remembered the six men he had seen leaving the airstrip and scoured the jungle for others.

The Indian darted to another tree. His actions betrayed he knew where the warrior was perched and was moving in for the kill.

Taking aim with the Whitworth, Bolan touched his finger to the trigger. The Indian broke from concealment, weaving as he ran. Bolan let him come a little closer, then the Express boomed and the Indian was punched to the earth.

Suddenly the darkness was torn by the angry rattle of automatic fire. Slugs smacked into the limbs above Bolan and the trunk underneath him. He ducked, saw several forms zeroing in on him from different directions and knew he had to get out of there. Coiling his legs, he leaped.

The ground was soft, cushioned by a layer of rotting leaves and grass. Even so, the ten-foot drop threw Bolan off balance and he rolled, inadvertently saving his life as rounds tore into the exact spot where he'd landed.

With a shove the warrior was up and sprinting westward. He had to find a defensible position or some way of losing the hardmen so he could circle around and retrieve the duffel.

Beside a vine-covered tree Bolan paused to look back. An arrow half the length of his body whizzed past his head by the barest margin and buried itself in the trunk with such force it quivered loudly. He ducked around the tree, bent low and ran on.

Bolan had no illusions about what he was up against. His jungle survival skills were considerable, but when compared to those of the Indians of the Mato Grosso, he was like a babe in the woods. The Indians were at home in the wilderness. They spent their whole lives there, honing their woodlore until they could track anything, anywhere. They were adept hunters, able to move as quietly as the fierce predators they competed with. And he had one, maybe more, on his tail.

Farther on the warrior veered to the right and squatted behind a forest giant. The Whitworth went over his back. With the Uzi in hand, he surveyed the undergrowth. Suddenly another arrow whizzed out of the gloom, striking the earth at his feet. Pivoting, he sought the archer but saw only trees.

The game of cat and mouse continued as Bolan retreated deeper into the jungle. Twice more the warrior tried to ambush his adversaries. Each time an arrow nearly clipped him. After the second incident he grew suspicious. Was the Indian missing him on purpose? he wondered. The idea seemed ridiculous, yet so was the notion that someone who had been using a bow since he was old enough to lift one couldn't hit a man-size target from close range, even in the dark.

Minutes later Bolan skirted a tangle of undergrowth and started across a small clearing. Abruptly his boots sank into mushy soil, and moisture soaked his ankles. Quicksand! Yanking his feet free, he straightened and went around to the left.

Ahead the jungle suddenly ended. Bolan spied what appeared to be a flat plain until he was close enough to see the reflections of stars on the glassy surface and note scattered islands of plant growth. A bit nearer and he smelled the water.

Now the warrior understood. The men on his heels hadn't been trying to kill him. They had been toying with him, leading him like a steer to the slaughter right to the edge of a trackless swamp. He turned, seeking to get out of there before they hemmed him in, but he was too late.

Not eight feet off stood a robust Indian, an arrow notched to his long bow, the barbed point centered on the warrior's chest.

15

The Executioner knew he couldn't lift the Uzi and fire before the Indian released the arrow. He also knew the Indian could have killed him at any time, yet hadn't. So he froze, waiting for the man to make the next move. Instead, a voice addressed him from the trees.

"*Senhor,* you will drop your guns and come with us, yes? Our boss wants a word with you."

Now Bolan understood why he was still alive. Carlos Cordoba wanted to pay him back for all he had done. He'd be tortured until he was on the verge of death, then dipped in acid and his body left in the jungle to rot.

"You must do as we say," the accented voice declared. "You have nowhere to go other than into the swamp, and no one lives long there."

Bolan stared at the Indian. The man's hair was cropped into the shape of a bowl, and his only article of clothing was a brief loincloth.

"If you do not obey, Yarulla will put that arrow into your heart."

"All right," Bolan said. He held the Uzi out, showing he was going to do as they wanted.

The gunner in the bushes spoke in a native dialect and Yarulla answered.

"We are waiting, *senhor.*"

"Here it is," Bolan declared. He made as if to throw the Uzi to the ground but flung the submachine gun at the Indian's face while simultaneously stepping to the right.

Automatically Yarulla shifted aside and loosed his arrow, which came so close it snatched at the warrior's shirt. Swiftly the Indian reached behind him for another.

Bolan beat him to the punch. The .45 sprang clear and he centered the barrel and stroked the trigger three times. Yarulla fell. Then muzzle-flashes blazed in the jungle, slugs nipping at Bolan's clothes as he whirled and dived. The tepid, rank water closed over his head, nearly making him gag, and he stroked with all his power, slanting deeper the farther he went. The weight of the Express slowed him down, the sling dragging on his neck.

The warrior swam until his lungs were ready to rupture, then arched upward and sucked in fresh air. To his rear the hardmen were raking the swamp with gunfire at random. He heard a shout, then ducked under and swam.

When next Bolan broke for a breath he was close to a tiny island. The gunners had lost sight of him and were yelling in confusion. Moving around the island, he gripped handfuls of weeds and pulled himself onto firm ground. Almost immediately mosquitoes swarmed around his head, biting his exposed skin.

The warrior rose high enough to peer at the shore and saw two men directly across from him and two others moving to the east. He shoved the Para-Ordnance in its shoulder holster and unslung the rifle. Taking a bead on one of the figures, he had the man set in his sights when there was a shout and all four vanished into the jungle.

Now what was that all about? Bolan speculated. He bided his time to see if they would come back, and when fifteen minutes had gone by he crept to the near side of his sanctuary and poised next to the water.

The warrior swatted at the annoying mosquitoes, then slipped back into the swamp. He tried not to think of the many poisonous snakes inhabiting South America as he paddled slowly along.

Once Bolan had solid ground under him he darted into the undergrowth. As yet there was no sign of the quartet, which mystified him no end. They simply wouldn't give up and leave, not when they had him trapped.

Another quarter of an hour elapsed and finally Bolan was convinced the gunners had gone. Standing, he searched for the Uzi but couldn't find it. Figuring the gunners had taken it with them, he craned his neck to study the sky. By the position of the Southern Cross he pinpointed his exact location in relation to the fortress and headed in that direction.

The warrior had covered a short distance when his instincts warned him that he wasn't alone. Halting, he listened to the chirp of insects and the distant screech of a monkey. No other sounds broke the rhythm of the jungle, so he advanced with his senses primed.

In a short while Bolan heard a rustling noise to the east. He was certain he was being shadowed, but was it by man or beast? A hillock offered him a chance to scan the countryside, and he trotted to the crest.

It was like being in the middle of a vast ocean of aquamarine that stretched to the four points of the compass. To the southwest a yellow glow signified the estate still burned. Bolan walked in a circle, monitoring the shadows. After a while he resumed hiking, and although he had no proof, he was still positive he was being stalked.

Soon movement to the right confirmed the warrior's belief. He spotted a man slinking on a parallel course and brought the Whitworth to bear. When the man melted into the background, Bolan went after him, zigzagging from tree to tree. He came to where he thought the man had been and saw no one. Venturing farther, he stopped next to a wide bole and wiped the back of a hand across his perspiring brow.

It was then that two Indians pounced, one coming around the tree to take Bolan from the rear while the other charged into the open from the front, brandishing a machete.

Iron bands constricted Bolan's chest, pinning his right arm to his side. Their plan was obvious. While one held him, the other would separate his head from his body.

Instinctively Bolan snapped his head backward, crunching his skull against the Indian's nose. The grip on his chest slackened a little. The warrior made it slacken even more by ramming his free elbow into the Indian's ribs. Then the one with the machete was front and center, swiping at Bolan's stomach. Only by pushing off with both legs and causing the Indian who held him to stumble backward did Bolan evade the keen blade.

The machete stabbed forward again. Bolan dug in his left heel and twisted sharply, throwing all his weight into the motion. The Indian holding him was caught unawares and was swung clear around—into the path of the machete.

The blade bit deep into the man's side. Releasing his hold, he pressed his hands to the spurting wound and staggered to the rear.

For a moment the man wielding the machete stood frozen with shock.

In that moment Bolan took a short step and jumped into the air, performing a flawless flying kick that smashed into Machete's jaw and sent the man reeling. He closed before the Indian could recover and rammed a snap kick to the knee. There was a crack, the Indian buckled and Bolan arced a knee to the mouth that left his adversary flat on his back.

Whirling, Bolan sought the wounded Indian and was startled to find him gone. As he took a step to pick up the rifle, the brush nearby crackled and four figures appeared.

"Izarari, did you get him?" someone called out in Portuguese.

Bolan couldn't reach the Whitworth before they realized their mistake and opened fire. In a cross draw he cleared the Para-Ordnance and the Tanarmi and leveled both pistols. In unison the .45 and the 9 mm cracked their litany of death, a steady cadence that made the bodies of the gunners jerk and twitch to its lethal tune. One of the gunners managed to snap off a short burst that went wild. Then all the hardmen were down and Bolan advanced, pumping bullets into those who still moved.

At last the warrior stopped firing. He ejected the spent clips and replaced them with new ones. Going from body to body, he made sure all the men were dead. Once that was done, he holstered the pistols and gathered all the hardware he could find.

Walking to where the Whitworth lay, Bolan deposited his load and sorted through the various subguns and pistols, debating which to take. He found his mini-Uzi. He also came across another Sten, this one a sound-suppressed version, and claimed it for his own.

When, shortly thereafter, the warrior hastened toward the villa, his pockets were crammed with all the 9 mm ammunition he could carry. The Express and the Uzi were slung over his back, the Sten Mark II in his hands. Unfortunately none of the gunners had carried grenades.

Bolan thought about the last two Indians he had killed, wondering where they had come from and why they had tried to kill him. Just a short while ago the one at the swamp had tried to take him alive.

As far as the Executioner knew, six men had left the airstrip to hunt him down, two Indians and four gunners. He'd killed one of the Indians back near the estate, the second near the swamp. He recalled seeing four men on the shore and then hearing a shout that had drawn them off.

Had two more Indians been sent by Cordoba? If so, why? To help the first pair track him? He considered the time frame and a possible answer occurred to him.

The original six had been sent right after the planes were blown. Cordoba had wanted him alive then, but that was before Bolan launched his rocket attack on the fortress. The arms lord had to have become so enraged he'd changed his mind and sent two more Indians to overtake the tracking party and inform them to eliminate Bolan at any cost. It was the only thing that made sense.

Bolan picked up the pace. Within the hour he was once again perched in the fork of the tree near the fortress wall. The first thing he noticed was that all the floodlights were out, that in fact there wasn't a light anywhere on the entire estate. The shattered ruins of the generator shack explained why.

Not so easily explained was the unnatural quiet. And even more puzzling was the fact there wasn't a soul anywhere. The fortress appeared deserted.

The warrior sat and watched for half an hour. He planned to stay there until daylight, then conduct a hard probe. But then he heard a scream, so faint it was barely audible, so filled with undiluted terror that Bolan's stomach muscles involuntarily tightened. The scream wavered on the breeze, going on and on. When it died, Bolan sprang to life.

Tossing down the duffel and now useless LAW pack, Bolan climbed to the ground. Since it was unwise to be burdened with unnecessary weight in a firefight, he left them there and moved toward the section of the wall demolished by his rocket. There was no movement in the guard tower. No one challenged him or opened fire.

Bolan picked his way past the rubble, keeping his back to the wall. Once inside, the full magnitude of the destruction was apparent. An enormous crater marked where the metal warehouse had stood. Every other building had sustained severe damage. Sections of the villa farthest from the blast radius still stood, but the walls were cracked and partially buckled. Dozens of bodies littered the estate.

The warrior took every precaution as he worked his way to the front wall. He saw the gate suspended at a slant, hanging open by one hinge.

Beyond, the night was still. Bolan paused, trying to deduce where the survivors had gone, when from the vicinity of the river came the report of a single shot.

Sprinting to the jungle, Bolan hurried toward the docks. He was still sixty feet away when he heard gruff laughter. Slowing, he crouched and approached cautiously. It took a few seconds for him to comprehend the sight he beheld, and when he did, his features became rock hard.

Eleven gunners were still alive. They were clustered around two roaring fires, some eating from tin cans. A single speedboat was tied to the ravaged docks. But it was the scene to the left of the fires that jarred the warrior.

Five people had been stripped, staked out and killed in the most horrible fashion; their skin had been sliced from their bodies, their eyes had been gouged out. Although their faces were unrecognizable, it was plain that four of them had been grown men and one a boy.

Bolan gazed at the speedboat, pained by the self-evident truth. The prisoners had come back for him. They should have been speeding to safety downriver, but they had been unable to abandon him and had returned only to be jumped by the hardmen and made to pay the supreme price for resisting Carlos Cordoba.

The warrior glanced around, seeking the arms lord. He was beginning to think the man had perished when the sadist and three more gunners appeared up the river and walked toward the fires.

One of the newcomers had a radio on his back. He removed the receiver, spoke briefly, and handed the receiver to Cordoba, who talked at some length.

Bolan couldn't hear many of the words. From the snatches he did make out, he gathered more boats were on their way and would be there by daylight. Little did Cordoba know that he wasn't going to live that long.

The warrior set down the Sten and unlimbered the Whitworth Express. He placed his elbows flat and was elevating the rifle when footsteps alerted him to the proximity of another gunner, a guard who was patrolling along the edge of the trees.

Bolan ducked low and saw a tall man wearing a wide-brimmed hat go by. When the coast was clear he focused on Cordoba and was vexed to find the weapons czar had gone to the speedboat and stepped in. Before Bolan could take aim, the arms lord disappeared from sight.

Expecting Cordoba to shortly reappear, Bolan lowered his cheek to the rifle. Minutes crawled by, however, and still no Cordoba. He saw the guards make themselves comfortable on the dock and realized he was in for a long wait. The arms lord had apparently gone onto the boat to catch some sleep.

Bolan had no recourse but to bide his time. He wasn't about to throw his life away by trying to get past the gunners to reach Cordoba. In due course he would get the clear shot he needed and the Vulture's brutal reign of terror would be ended once and for all.

The warrior crossed his arms and rested his chin on his wrist. He might as well get some rest, too. He'd need to be fully alert come morning.

The drone of buzzing insects had a relaxing effect. He dozed off but slept fitfully, waking often to check on the status of the camp. Only about half of the gunners had stretched out on the ground. The remainder were too excited by the events of the day to sleep.

A PALE GLOW LIGHTED the sky when the rumble of engines arose downriver. Instantly the camp was alert, the gunners rising and moving to the water's edge. Cordoba also awakened and waited in the speedboat.

The Executioner tried to fix his sights on the arms lord, but too many hardmen stood between them.

A pair of speedboats zoomed into view, prompting a cheer from the gunners. The new arrivals coasted to the docks, and Cordoba issued orders, dividing the men up. Four were assigned to each craft. He picked those for his own boat first. Consequently he was loaded and pulling out well before the others.

Cordoba would get away unless the Executioner moved quickly. Standing, he slung the rifle, scooped up the Sten and sprinted from hiding.

The gunners were too busy piling onto the craft to notice. A second boat pulled out. The last man, the guard in the wide-brimmed hat, was about to hop onto the third boat when one of his companions spotted the warrior and gave a yell.

By then Bolan was close enough to use the Sten. He raked the boat, his first burst catching the guard in the chest and flipping the man back into the others. All of them fell in a jumble of arms and legs, except for the man at the wheel. He pivoted, bringing up a pistol.

The Sten coughed several more times and the boat's operator was thrown against the wheel. Bolan reached the side of the boat and cored the brain of a gunner pointing a Walther MPL. Only two hardmen were alive, one pinned under the dead guard, the second tugging at the strap of a slung Skorpion. Both crumpled at Bolan's next burst.

Because the Sten was fitted with a suppressor, none of the shots was heard by the retreating boats. One of the gunners in the second craft had seen Bolan, though, and was doing his best imitation of a town crier. The boat began to come around.

Bolan jumped onto the third vessel, shoved the operator aside and checked the controls. Everything appeared to be in order. Opening the throttle, he shot out onto the river and steered to starboard in an effort to swing around the second boat and go after Cordoba.

The man handling the second boat wasn't about to allow the warrior to slip past. Gunning his engine, he steered on an intercept heading. The gunners in his boat opened up.

Bolan ducked as his windshield shuddered under multiple impacts. He repeatedly slewed right, then left, creating a wash that rocked the other boat, slowing them. Gradually he pulled ahead and the hardmen ceased firing.

The first craft had already gone around the bend. When Bolan negotiated the turn he saw Cordoba's speedboat a quarter of a mile off, racing along at top speed.

A speaker on the console blared to life as the operator of the third boat contacted Cordoba's. There was a flurry in Portuguese, then a long pause. The next words were in English.

"My congratulations, whoever you are. You have more lives than a cat."

Bolan kept his hands on the wheel as he pushed the speedboat to its limits.

"I know you can hear me," Cordoba said confidently. "Pick up the mike."

The warrior glanced at it but didn't.

"All I want is for you to hear me out. What harm can it do you?"

Frowning, Bolan made contact. "There's nothing you can say that can possibly interest me."

"You haven't heard my proposition yet," Cordoba replied, sounding relieved that Bolan had answered.

"Save your breath."

"Are you that dedicated? Or are you just a fool? I can make you a very rich man, richer than your wildest dreams."

Bolan expected a pitch, and he wasn't disappointed.

"I must compliment you on your resourcefulness," the arms lord went on. "Who would have believed that one man could cause so much trouble, eh? By yourself you have done what the combined police forces of several countries have been unable to do. You are a formidable enemy."

His gaze glued to the river, Bolan made no reply.

"You can tell me now. Are you CIA? Some other agency? What?" Cordoba was silent a minute, then continued. "All right. Don't talk to me. Just listen." There was a low cough. "I admit you have brought my operation to a standstill and destroyed most of my munitions. But I can easily start over. I still have millions in the bank, and I am not a selfish man. How would you like a share of my wealth?"

Pathetic, Bolan mused.

"I am sincere, *senhor*," Cordoba said quickly, as if guessing the warrior's reaction. "I will pay you the sum of half a million dollars. All you have to do is let me escape. What do you say? Half a million dollars for doing nothing. How easy can making money be?"

"Save your millions for your funeral," Bolan replied. "You can go out in style."

"Half a million dollars means nothing to you? Very well. I will pay you a million dollars. What do you say?"

"I've heard all this before."

"Are you insane? You would give up a chance to live in luxury for the rest of your life? Think, *senhor.*"

"I think you're running scared, Cordoba. I think you're trying to buy me off as a last resort."

"What does it matter why I am doing it? The money will still be yours."

Bolan veered to avoid a log. "I've been offered deals like this before and my answer is always the same."

"You would rather be poor than wealthy?"

"I would rather sleep better at night knowing there is one less mad dog running loose, one less killer who goes around butchering innocents and spreading terrorism throughout the world."

Static crackled for a few seconds. "I can see there is no reasoning with you. You are a fanatic. So I will deal with you as I should have dealt with you the first minute I set eyes on you."

"You'll try," Bolan corrected him, and the link went dead. Bolan hung up the mike, then glanced back. So far he was holding his own. The third speedboat hadn't narrowed the gap, indeed had fallen a few hundred feet farther behind.

For the next forty minutes the status quo was maintained. Cordoba held his substantial lead. Bolan doggedly pursued. Then a new element was added to the equation when the speaker hissed and the arms czar came on.

"I have some bad news for you, *senhor.* Before you destroyed my satellite, I was able to get off two messages. One was a request for boats to be sent. The other—'' Cordoba laughed. ''Perhaps you should turn your eyes to the eastern sky.''

Bolan looked.

Winging toward them was a warplane.

16

Mack Bolan didn't waste precious time speculating on where the warbird came from. It didn't matter whether the aircraft belonged to Cordoba or had been sent by one of the arms lord's cronies in the military. All that concerned Bolan was his vulnerable position in the middle of the river. So when he saw a narrow tributary to his right, he curved toward its mouth.

The aircraft went into a strafing run. It reminded Bolan of an old T-28, a World War Two propeller job, the kind bought by collectors yearning to relive the glory days of fighter planes.

Bolan gauged the distance to the tributary against the speed of the oncoming aircraft and knew he wouldn't reach cover in time. Quickly he brought the Whitworth Express into play. Using a rifle against an airplane was tantamount to using a peashooter against an eagle, but it was all he had. He aimed at the propeller.

The fighter shrieked out of the sky like a banshee gone berserk, the pilot bringing the plane in so low he nearly skimmed the water. Wing-mounted machine guns chattered, and a path of miniature geysers closed on the speedboat.

Bolan banged off a shot, then grabbed the wheel and wrenched it to the left. He heard the heavy-caliber slugs tear into the rear of the speedboat. A look showed a number of holes but no water seeping in. Yet.

The fighter banked and climbed, gaining altitude for another run.

The warrior swept into the tributary, alert for obstacles. Trees overhung the water on both banks, some jutting twenty feet or more. He steered to the right, under the comforting canopy, and slowed to a standstill.

Seconds later the fighter roared overhead, the pilot slanting the plane to get a better view. It streaked off to the east, then soared on high again.

For the moment, at least, Bolan was safe. Eventually the pilot would spot the boat and he'd have to make a run for it. And there was no deluding himself. He couldn't hope to outrun the warbird, and he certainly couldn't outgun her. He'd either be blown out of the water or stranded in the jungle miles from the nearest outpost.

A branch hanging low over the windshield suggested a third possibility. Letting the speedboat idle, Bolan grasped the branch, tested it by pulling with all his might and jumped. The limb sagged but held, and Bolan was able to go up hand over hand to a sturdier branch. From there he climbed to the trunk, then went up.

Suddenly the warplane made its third run, zipping mere yards above the treetops.

Bolan stayed still until the fighter arced skyward once more. Hurrying, he climbed steadily higher, to the upper terrace where the limbs were so small they could barely support his weight, until he was five feet below the top of the tree.

Balancing precariously, the warrior poked his head up and scanned the sky. Sunlight shimmering off the fighter's wings pinpointed its location, about half a mile to the southeast, angling for another dive. He sat, locked one leg around the bole and hastily replaced the magazine in the Sten. Then, craning his neck, he focused on the warbird.

The pilot was a risk taker. He came in low, as before, only slower, looking right and left.

Bolan had to compensate for the plane's speed by tracking in front of it. He held his fire when he saw that the fighter would pass sixty yards to the south of his position. The pilot evidently had no idea he had stopped and believed he was heading up the tributary.

Three more times the warplane made passes, each time farther south. Bolan hoped the pilot would give up and leave, but the man was persistent. The fighter looped and swooped almost directly toward him.

Quickly Bolan sighted, led the plane by a dozen yards and squeezed the trigger when he judged it to be within range. He had to have hit something, because the aircraft abruptly flashed up into the blue.

On the next pass the pilot was all business. He dived, his machine guns blazing, chewing up the foliage. His sense of direction was uncanny, because he was only feet shy of the tree in which the warrior perched.

Bolan emptied the Sten's magazine as the warplane thundered by. He thought he saw sparks fly and heard slugs whine off the fuselage. Then the fighter was up and away again, climbing for another strafing run.

The warrior slapped another magazine into the Sten, then leaned back for a better firing angle. This time the pilot had his position pegged, and the aircraft screeched toward him like a great bird of prey. Bolan mentally ticked off the yards. The fighter's machine guns opened up, and all around him limbs and leaves were blasted to pieces. He waited until the very last moment and tucked the trigger tight.

The warplane shuddered. Smoke billowed from under the engine cowling. In the blink of an eye the fighter had passed and the pilot soared to gain altitude.

Bolan expected the plane to leave. Ominous black smoke poured from under the stricken aircraft, and the wings were wobbling as if the pilot were having a difficult time holding her steady. He started down, then stopped on seeing the fighter go into one more dive.

The warrior had no more loaded magazines for the Sten. He switched to the mini-Uzi and was taking aim when the airplane tilted sharply to the south. He could see the pilot desperately fighting the stick. It was a losing battle.

Two hundred yards off the fighter suddenly lost flight capability and plummeted. A great explosion rocked the jungle when the warplane hit, and a mushroom-shaped column of fire seared high into the air.

Bolan didn't stay to watch the aircraft burn. He scrambled down the tree and dropped into the speedboat. Powering up, he made an abrupt U-turn and sped back to the Sucuriú River. By now the other two speedboats were long out of sight.

There was only one chance of catching them. The warrior had to lighten his load to get extra speed. He did so by tossing the slain gunners overboard and casting out every nonessential item. Then he turned into the main channel and let the boat fly.

Spray moistened Bolan's face. The wind fanned his hair. He squinted against the glare and held the throttle wide open.

A straight stretch of five miles enabled Bolan to pull out all the stops. Ahead the surface was tranquil, showing he was ten minutes or more behind Cordoba's boats. He couldn't tolerate the thought of the arms lord escaping, and every few minutes he shielded his eyes with a palm and stared into the distance in the hope of spotting his quarry.

In due time devastated Taguarí appeared on the warrior's right. The inhabitants had returned and were rebuilding their shanties. Some stopped work to stare at the speedboat. The only craft tied at the shore was a raft.

Onward Bolan went, the sun climbing steadily higher, his fuel gauge steadily dropping. At the speed he was going, he figured to run out of gas in less than an hour. The next town, if he remembered correctly, was a small settlement called Boa Nova. To reach it he would have to cut back the throttle and nurse his remaining fuel, and although he didn't like slowing down, that was what he did.

By the warrior's reckoning he was still five miles from Boa Nova when he came around a bend and spied another speedboat on the east shore. Bringing his vessel to a crawl, he picked up the Whitworth and scanned the area where the boat was beached. It looked deserted, but Bolan wasn't about to be lured into a trap. He circled offshore, bending low in case there were snipers hidden in the trees.

An oil slick told Bolan why the speedboat had been abandoned. He nosed his boat closer and saw a large black smudge on the other craft. The engine had blown out, and Cordoba had to have taken the gunners onto the first boat and kept on downriver.

Bolan revved his engine and headed out in pursuit. There were now ten men on the arms lord's craft, far too many for so small a boat. They would be limping along to conserve fuel. With a bit of luck he might overtake them before they reached Boa Nova.

Presently the town came into sight. Bolan saw a score of various canoes, rafts and other vessels moored at the rickety docks, prominent among them Cordoba's speedboat. He steered close to the bank and approached at a snail's pace.

Boa Nova was bigger than Taguarí had been. There might be police, so it wouldn't do for Bolan to stroll through the streets armed for bear. A hundred yards from the edge of town he killed the engine and let the speedboat coast to a stop behind a bank that jutted into the river.

He secured the mooring line, then hid the Whitworth and the Sten in bushes. He stripped off both shoulder holsters, pulled out his shirttail and wedged the two pistols under his belt behind his back. Next he removed the suppressor from the mini-Uzi and tucked the weapon under the front of his shirt.

Hiking southward, the warrior soon came on a well-worn trail that led to town. He had gone a short way when an elderly couple appeared, leading a burro. Bolan stopped, noticing the man's straw sombrero. He checked in his pocket and found he still had a wad of money. When the couple neared him he peeled off several large bills, held the money out and pointed at the hat. "I'd like to buy that."

The couple halted, their surprise evident. They whispered a bit, the man shaking his head and the woman jabbing a finger at the bills. At last a compromise was reached and the warrior owned a sombrero.

Bolan smiled and waved as he walked off. He pulled the front brim of the hat low enough to cover the upper half of his face. In less than a minute he emerged into a field. Several people were nearby, chopping wood. They ignored him as he crossed to a rutted side street and entered Boa Nova.

As in Taguarí, most of the dwellings were little better than flimsy hovels. But there were a few sturdier structures. On the main street there were two bars, a post office and a church built in the last century.

Bolan stuck to the shadows as he prowled, in order to be inconspicuous. A few curious stares were directed his way, otherwise he was left alone. He saw no police, but on coming around a corner close to one of the bars he spotted three of Cordoba's hardmen standing outside the entrance with their subguns in hand.

The warrior stopped, turned his back to them and leaned against the wall. Twisting his head, he peeked out from under the sombrero. The gunners hadn't spotted him. They were too busy guzzling beer and joking.

Where were the rest? Bolan wondered. More important, where was Cordoba? He squatted and slid a hand under his shirt to grasp the small Uzi.

Shortly two more gunners came out of the bar, and all of them moved off down the street. A young woman trying to get by them was jostled and groped. When she broke into tears, the hardmen laughed.

Standing, Bolan followed at a discreet distance. The five men ambled to the other bar and went in. The warrior ducked into an alley, intending to go in by the back way, but there was no rear door. Stymied, he returned to the main street and crouched at the corner of a building.

He didn't wait long. Cordoba walked into the sunshine trailed by his nine hardmen. They turned right, moving down the center of the street.

Too many innocents were abroad for Bolan to risk starting a gun battle. He shadowed Cordoba, hanging far back.

The arms lord stopped at a house and knocked. A man answered and a short talk ensued. Cordoba handed over some money, the man nodded, then motioned for them to tag along as he headed toward the river.

Bolan was caught flat-footed. He was in front of a building with nowhere to hide. To his right was a wooden barrel. He took two steps and sank down beside it, pulling his legs up to his chest and bending his head so the sombrero screened his face. The tromp of feet told him Cordoba's men were getting closer, and he braced himself for an outcry that would result in a bloodbath. All he heard were gruff voices and a chuckle.

The warrior sat there until the footsteps receded, stood and dogged the pack of killers once more. They headed for the docks, to a locked shed east of where the boats were tied. The man Cordoba had paid produced a key, unlocked the shed and brought out four ten-liter gas cans which he gave to the hardmen.

Now Bolan understood what was going on. Cordoba wanted extra fuel so he wouldn't have to stop again until he was halfway to Rio. Judging by the way his men were holding the cans, they were already full.

The warrior couldn't allow them to leave. He watched as the cans were loaded onto the speedboat. Cordoba walked to the end of the plank wharf and stared up the Sucuriú. He also checked his watch, then scoured the sky. It was obvious he was wondering about the plane.

Bolan crept nearer, to the side of a shack twenty feet from the water's edge. The only other people in sight were three Indians unloading bales of long leaves from a canoe. He pulled out the Uzi and held it at his side, mentally willing the Indians to get out of the way. But they were in no rush.

The weapons czar walked back to his men. One of them spoke and patted his stomach.

Meanwhile the Indians had lifted their bales onto their shoulders and were trudging into Boa Nova. The moment they were in the clear, the Executioner stepped into the open, swung the Uzi up and fired. At the same instant one of the hardmen saw him and gave Cordoba a shove while shouting a warning.

Bolan's initial burst would have ripped into the arms lord's back if not for the loyal gunner, who took the brunt of the slugs himself. Cordoba fell prone as his startled men frantically brought their hardware into action.

A hailstorm of lead drove Bolan back behind the shed. He dropped to his knees with wood splintering and showering on him, then dived outward, onto his stomach, and sent a second burst into the clustered hardmen. Two more toppled. The rest spread out, their subguns chattering.

Bolan scrabbled under cover. The shed was being chipped to pieces. He had to keep the killers at bay or a random round was bound to find a vital organ.

Poking the Uzi around the corner, the warrior emptied the magazine in a swift sweep, felling a fourth gunner and forcing the rest to flatten or die. He glimpsed Cordoba vaulting into the speedboat and tried to peg him with the last few shots in the magazine. But the man stumbled, falling to his hands and knees, and the shots went high.

There was a shallow ditch a few yards to the rear of the shed. Bolan sprinted for it, replacing the magazine as he ran. He slid over the edge, landed in rank, filthy brown water and spun. A trio of gunners was in a headlong rush to the shed. They didn't realize he had shifted position until the Uzi pointed out their error.

Now only three men were left besides Cordoba. Bolan heard the engine sputtering as he traded shots. From the sound of things, the arms lord had flooded it.

One more hardman was put out of action. The remaining pair decided discretion was the better part of valor and bolted toward Boa Nova.

Bolan surged up out of the ditch, sighted down the Uzi and fired a long burst. Both gunners sprawled to the turf and were still.

The Executioner turned as the speedboat thundered to life. Cordoba was the proverbial sitting duck, and the warrior closed his finger around the trigger. But there were no rapid-fire reports. The Uzi had gone empty.

Suddenly the speedboat launched straight ahead. Bolan couldn't change magazines fast enough to get off a burst, but he was near enough to take a running dive for the tail end of the craft. He let go of the Uzi as he leaped, his arms outstretched. By the width of a hair he missed and landed in the river. As he hit the water he saw the mooring line, which Cordoba had neglected to cast off. It stretched taut, snapped and snaked after the boat, shooting right past Bolan.

Lunging, the warrior seized hold with both hands and held on with all his strength as the speedboat bore to the right and gained speed, dragging him in its wake. Water cascaded over him, getting into his nose, his mouth. Holding his breath, he ducked his head low, submerged himself as at the same time he hauled himself forward hand over hand.

When Bolan came up for air, he was halfway to the transom. Cordoba was laughing in triumph while glancing back at the docks. He didn't spot Bolan, and when Cordoba faced front, the warrior pulled himself closer, resisting the constant pressure of the buffeting water.

Bolan's shoulders ached when at length he gripped the top edge of the transom with his right hand. He hooked his left arm onto the boat, then, his teeth clamped, laboriously pulled himself out of the river.

The extra weight alerted the arms lord, who took one look over his shoulder, snarled like an animal and attacked, forgetting all about the wheel in his lust for vengeance.

The warrior rose to meet the charge and aimed a karate kick at Cordoba's neck, but his soaked shoe found no purchase on the smooth bottom and his left foot slipped out from under him before the blow could connect.

Cordoba took a little hop and came down feet-first on Bolan's midsection. The warrior winced, then twisted and shoved, upending Cordoba, who thudded down next to him.

Clawed fingers closed on Bolan's windpipe. He tried ripping Cordoba's hands off, but the arms lord fought like a madman, his nails digging deeper and deeper. Bolan rammed a fist into his adversary's ribs, and the arms czar tried to head-butt him in the face.

Without warning, the out-of-control speedboat swerved, causing the warrior and Cordoba to roll, pitching them against the port gunwale. Bolan took the brunt of the impact and found himself pinned. He lashed out, a bone-crunching punch to the mouth that pulped his enemy's lips.

Bolan got both hands on his foe's shoulders and pushed. He managed to force Cordoba to arm's length. The arms lord's eyes widened, then they filled with terror.

The next moment Bolan learned why. The speedboat plowed into the east shore, hitting an incline that propelled the vessel up and over the bank and into the jungle. The din of shattering branches and broken bushes reminded Bolan of the amphibian crash.

Suddenly the speedboat hit something and became airborne. Like an oversize javelin it arched skyward, then the bow canted and it smashed into the ground.

Bolan and Cordoba were flung apart. The warrior smacked into a jumbled web of creepers and limbs that cushioned his descent. He bounced off a stout branch, struck a tree trunk and wound up on his side in a patch of weeds, battered and bruised but intact.

The warrior's legs wobbled as he stood. Nearby the speedboat was a shattered mockery of its former shape. He glanced right, saw the river forty feet away, then glanced left and saw Cordoba fleeing into the jungle.

The warrior gave chase, reaching behind him for a pistol. Both the .45 and the 9 mm were gone, either at the bottom of the river or lost in the vegetation. He would have to take Cordoba hand to hand.

The arms lord glanced around, roared in anger and tripped. Before he could stand, Bolan was on him. Cordoba grasped a fallen branch and swung. Bolan skipped aside, then delivered a stamping kick to his adversary's instep that threw the man off balance.

Tottering rearward, Cordoba reversed his grip on the branch and drove the tapered end at Bolan's chest. The warrior used a forearm block to deflect the thrust and streaked a crescent kick into Cordoba's stomach.

The arms lord went down, but only to his knees. He speared the branch at his enemy's groin, but Bolan twisted and the branch missed.

The Executioner lanced a ridge-hand blow into the side of Cordoba's neck. Knocked sideways, the arms lord gamely tried to raise the branch again. Quickly the warrior stepped in close, gripped Cordoba by the hair and yanked the man's head back.

Four times Bolan's right arm flashed, four times the hard edge of his hand knifed into Cordoba's throat. He let go, and the arms lord swayed, his eyes bulging, his face bright red. Inarticulate sounds sputtered from Cordoba's lips. Then, eyelids fluttering, he pitched over, wheezed, and died.

The Executioner took a deep breath and exhaled slowly. At long last it was over. Justice had been served, and the thousands of innocents the Vulture had sent to early graves could rest easy in the hereafter.

Bolan turned and headed toward Boa Nova. He would retrieve the speedboat and in two days be back in Rio. In three he would be in America.

Home.

And ready to carry on the good fight.

**Bolan is in attack mode in the final
Irish killing fields**

DON PENDLETON's
MACK BOLAN.

BLOOD STRIKE

The Sword of Erin, a renegade faction of the IRA, had
gambled with the lifeblood of their own movement when
they massacred federal agents in New York—and staged
the escape of the group's leader, William Connolly.

Take
4 explosive books
plus a
mystery bonus

FREE

**Don't miss out on the action in these titles featuring
THE EXECUTIONER®, ABLE TEAM® and PHOENIX FORCE®!**

The Terror Trilogy

Features Mack Bolan, along with ABLE TEAM and PHOENIX FORCE, as they
battle neo-Nazis and Arab terrorists to prevent war in the Middle East.

The Executioner #61186	FIRE BURST	$3.50 U.S.	☐
		$3.99 Can.	☐
The Executioner #61187	CLEANSING FLAME	$3.50 U.S.	☐
		$3.99 Can.	☐
SuperBolan #61437	INFERNO	$4.99 U.S.	☐
		$5.50 Can.	☐

The Executioner®

Nonstop action, as Mack Bolan represents ultimate justice, within or beyond
the law.

#61184	DEATH WARRANT	$3.50	☐
#61185	SUDDEN FURY	$3.50	☐

(limited quantities available on certain titles)

TOTAL AMOUNT	$
POSTAGE & HANDLING	$
($1.00 for one book, 50¢ for each additional)	
APPLICABLE TAXES*	$ _____
TOTAL PAYABLE	$ _____

(check or money order—please do not send cash)

To order, complete this form and send it, along with a check or money order for
the total above, payable to Gold Eagle Books, to: **In the U.S.:** 3010 Walden Avenue,
P.O. Box 9077, Buffalo, NY 14269-9077; **In Canada:** P.O. Box 636, Fort Erie, Ontario,
L2A 5X3.

Name:_____

Address:_____ City:_____

State/Prov.:_____ Zip/Postal Code: _____

*New York residents remit applicable sales taxes.
Canadian residents remit applicable GST and provincial taxes.

GEBACK8